ENHANCED

THE ENHANCED, BOOK ONE

T.C. EDGE

MW00439387

Copyright Notice

This book is a work of fiction. Any names, places, events, and incidents that occur are entirely a result of the author's imagination and any resemblance to real people, events, and places is entirely coincidental.

Copyright 2016 T. C. Edge

All right reserved.

First edition: December 2016

Cover Design by Laercio Messias

No part of this book may be scanned, reproduced, or distributed in any printed or electronic form.

To hear about the author's latest discounts and new releases, sign up to his newsletter at
www.tcedgebooks.com

TABLE OF CONTENTS

CHAPTER ONE

The sign above the door reads: *'Carmichael's Academy'*.

It's old and worn down, the metal rusted at the corners and hanging slightly loose on one side. Just from looking at it, you'd assume that the inside of the building was equally unkempt.

And you'd be right.

It's a lie too. The word 'academy' in the title makes the building appear more than it is. A place, perhaps, for study and work, where the young are taught and educated and given a vocation.

Really, it's little more than a refuge for orphans and castaways, one of the few remaining in the city. Were it not for Mrs Carmichael, most of the kids here would find themselves in the northern quarter, swallowed up by the alleys and joining the ranks of the Disposables.

It's a sorry truth that many will end up there anyway. Mrs Carmichael's charity can only stretch so far.

I step over the threshold from the bustling street of Brick Lane and enter inside. A smell I know so intimately sweeps up my nose, the pungent scent of unwashed clothes and tobacco smoke that refuses to give way despite my best efforts. I have made it my mission to dismiss the odour for a while now, but to no avail.

It's our generous patron herself who contributes to the stench. Despite her many excellent qualities, Mrs Carmichael is a heavy smoker, a habit that appears to have been taken on by some of the older tenants living here.

"It's a losing battle," she always tells me when she finds me scrubbing the old carpets and worn out curtains, puffing happily on a cigarette as she does so.

I usually just smile and keep going. Frankly, it's more as a way of keeping busy than anything else.

The academy, or orphanage – because that's what it really is – is situated over three floors in the west of Outer Haven, cosily nestled within one of the busiest residential districts in the city.

The ground floor is taken up by the youngsters, the kids who are unable to legally work. They perform tasks around the place, washing dishes and cleaning clothes. Given how that side of the stench refuses to leave, I consider that they're not doing a great job.

The first floor is occupied by those in transition. Kids of an age where they can find a vocation, and yet are unable to do so. They are given only so long before they find themselves on the other side of the door. It's harsh, but a necessary feature of life here at Carmichael's.

Such is the way throughout the sprawling urban jungle of Outer Haven.

The second and top floor, meanwhile, exists to house those old enough to work. Half the money they earn is used to help care for those on the floors below. The other half is held in trust by our patron until the time is right for them to fly the nest. Mostly, that happens when they're granted a housing license by the council and have a suitable pot of money to cover their essentials.

Overall, it's a symbiotic system where you work hard and give back. Since many of the kids here come when they're very young, they're only too happy to reciprocate when they reach the working age of 15.

Some, of course, have been here longer than others.

For me, it's all my life.

Eighteen years under the caring watch of Mrs Carmichael, the only parent I've ever known. I can honestly say it would take me a lifetime to repay her. If I could give her all of my wages, I would.

Up through the building I step, passing the dusty main hall and moving up the winding staircase that leads to the second floor. The smell of stale smoke grows stronger as I rise and move down the corridor to the rear of the building. At the end, Mrs Carmichael's own quarters await, with my room nearby on the left of the hallway.

My first port of call is to tap on her door.

My knuckles rap gently, and I hear a muffled call from within. I step inside and see my guardian sitting behind her desk in a fairly small and cluttered office. Off to the right, another door leads to her bedroom. On the left, she has a bathroom and little kitchenette. It's a meagre allotment, but something she's never cared for.

It's no surprise to find a cigarette dangling from her lips as she peruses some old files. Nor, given the time of day, is the sight of a large glass of whiskey particularly unusual.

Behind an old pair of horn-rimmed glasses, her murky blue eyes rise to mine, a web of grey hair dangling untidily from her head. I've noticed that her general interest in her appearance has declined since the death of her husband, Derek, several years ago.

"Evening, Brie," she croaks, her thin lips building into a smile as her spindly fingers take possession of the cigarette. "Update?"

"Yes, Mrs Carmichael," I say. "The job's all finished. The client was pleased. At least, I think he was."

"I'm sure he was, honey. Did you get payment?"

"Sure did," I say, stepping forward.

I reach into my jacket pocket and pull out an envelope. For the most part, we operate on a cash only basis around here, most of our jobs being kept off the books. Mrs Carmichael enjoys a certain degree of anonymity, and doesn't care for interference. Clearly, it works. I've never known anyone from the Court to venture this far. They don't tend to take much interest in the lower workings of Outer Haven.

She takes a grip of the envelope, has a cursory look inside to make sure everything looks right, and slips it into a coded safe in a drawer on the right of her desk. Then, taking a swig of whiskey, she looks back up at me.

"Tomorrow you're needed down at Culture Corner," she says. "Some Fanatics have been getting trigger happy with their graffiti again."

I know what that means. My role here involves doing odd-jobs, mostly menial stuff that, frankly, a trained monkey could happily handle. It's hardly fulfilling, but there you go. Few can boast of a particularly prosperous working life in this part of the city.

"Right. The same sort of stuff as before?" I ask.

She shrugs absentmindedly. "Most likely. I don't know the exact details. Just that you're needed down there at dawn, before the area becomes too busy. Tess will go with you, so pass on the message for me."

"OK, sure will."

Tess, my roommate and best friend, is at a similar stage to me here at the academy. She's about the same age, and we commonly find ourselves working together around the city. Unlike me, however, she has memories of her parents, who died when she

9

was just nine. I have no such burden.

Instead, I have a long list of questions that will probably never be answered. A thousand hours spent wondering about who they were and why they abandoned me. All I have to go on is what Mrs Carmichael told me: that I was found crying and alone in a bundle of blankets on her doorstep, with nothing but a picture tucked up beside me.

A picture of my mother and father, holding me as a baby. It's my only true link to the past.

Before I leave the room, Mrs Carmichael fixes me with a firm look.

"Have you taken your pills for the day?" she asks me.

For all the trust she's developed in me over the years, my ability to take my diabetes medication has remained a constant doubt in her mind. Every single day, without fail, she utters the same question, delivered with the same critical tone to her croaky voice.

And every time, I utter the same reply.

"Yes, Mrs Carmichael, of course I have," I say with a knowing smirk.

She offers a smile in return and falls into another of her most commonly asked questions.

"Are you ever going to start calling me Brenda?"

And, as always, I play to our usual script.

"One day, when I've repaid you enough," I answer.

It's a day I know will never come.

With a typical roll of the eyes, she shakes her head and gives off a raspy little laugh, before lighting up a fresh cigarette and returning her eyes to her files.

"Goodnight then, Brie," she mutters. "And remember, be down at Culture Corner by dawn."

I nod and exit the room, stepping back into the dim corridor with its moth eaten red carpet and creaking floorboards beneath. Down below, I can hear the sound of raucous play emanating from the ground floor. At this time of the evening, just before bed, some of the youngsters tend to get quite boisterous.

It's not quite the same up here, though. For the most part, everyone is exhausted by this point, and want little more than to sink into their beds and call it quits for the day. My own body is that way inclined, so I quickly make my way down the corridor and into my room.

Inside, I find Tess already in bed, lying face up on the left of the room just staring at the ceiling. She looks half comatose, her usually bright blue eyes blank and struggling to stay open as they linger on the peeling white paint above.

It's clearly been an exhausting day.

"Long day?" I ask her as I shut the door behind me.

Slowly, her head swivels to look at me. Her expression answers for her.

I laugh and begin undressing, peeling off the

utility clothes that I tend to wear most days with the sort of work I've been getting recently. They fall into a bundle on the floor as I enter my bedclothes and set about brushing my teeth.

With my mouth full of toothpaste, I tell Tess about tomorrow's job.

"We need to be at Culture Corner at dawn," I say.

I can hear her groan behind me.

"What sort of job?" she moans.

"Clean up, I guess," I tell her. "More graffiti from the Fanatics."

"Oh God, that stuff's a nightmare to get off."

"Tell me about it." I turn to her and note that she's still fully dressed and looking particularly bedraggled, her dirty blonde hair more murky than usual and her face spotted with dirt. She still looks pretty, though. That never seems to change. "You gonna, um, wash before bed?"

She grunts and shakes her head, before pulling a blanket over her body with some difficultly.

"What's the point," she mumbles, before rolling over and disappearing under the covers. "I'll just get dirty again."

I can't help but giggle at the sight. I've been there before plenty of times. It's nice to be on the other side of it for once.

Feeling relatively fresh, I turn off the main light and climb into bed, before pulling a little glowstick from my bedside table. I click a button and it emits a pale white glow that lights up only my side of the little room.

"I'll wake you before dawn," I say to Tess. "We can't be late."

I wait for a confirmative grunt before turning to the opposite wall, setting the glowstick down on the bed. It casts a soft light onto the bland wallpaper, bare brick showing in places where its cracked and torn.

But it's not the wall I'm looking at.

My eyes stare at two faces as I lie there, themselves worn down and fading now. My mother, warm brunette locks tied into a bun, holding me tenderly in her arms. My father, a strong arm curling around my mother's shoulder, his hazel eyes, just like mine, staring down at me.

It's a picture I've looked at every night since I can remember, my day somehow incomplete until I've inspected the image that seems so alien, so disconnected from my real world.

I often wonder how they could have left me behind, seeing the affection and love in their eyes as they look at me. And then I look a little closer, and note the pain there too, the undercurrent of heartbreak that hovers in their expressions.

And I realise that what they did, they did for a reason. And that, most likely, I'll never find out what it was.

CHAPTER TWO

My alarm begins blaring half an hour before dawn, ruthlessly dragging me out of a deep sleep.

An ingrained habit has me leaping straight out of bed, the chill of the morning creeping up my spine as I quickly jump back into my utility clothes; bland grey trousers and jacket, with an old t-shirt and jumper underneath for warmth, coupled with sturdy work boots that are less than flattering to a girl of 18.

As I dress, I call out for Tess to get up. Clearly, my alarm isn't enough for her.

"Tess, come on, rise and shine," I say, darting over to shake her awake.

When she refuses to budge for even a moment, I swiftly drag off her blanket and let the cool morning air sweep over her. Her eyes crack open and glare at me.

"I hate you," she mutters, before slowly standing to her feet.

"Love you too," comes my bright response, my hands busily tying my brown locks into a ponytail before brushing my teeth.

Tess follows me to the basin, wearily freshening

her breath before we hastily wolf down a couple of protein rich breakfast bars. They're bland and functional, supplying us with all the necessary energy we'll need to see through a hard morning's work.

Within 3 minutes of my frankly deafening alarm, we're up and ready to go, fully clothed and with our workbags tightly wrapped around our backs.

Together, we sweep down through the building towards the ground floor, everyone else still fast asleep. The same is largely true when we exit into the morning air, the sky still dark and the streets covered with an unpleasant mist.

There are few people on the streets, but their absence is made up for by the many drones hovering across the sky, their lights shining within the mist as they hurtle here and there. Most are postal drones, delivering goods and parcels before the world awakes. Others, however, are sentries, keeping an eye on us for their masters at the centre of Inner Haven.

Before hurrying into the mist, we set our sights a little way down the street at a large glowing post that sticks about 10 feet out of the ground. Currently, it's a fairly bright shade of green, indicating that the current fog isn't toxic. When that green turns to yellow, and then red, you know that it's time to get inside.

We move off down the street, heading south towards Culture Corner. When we arrive at a soon-to-be-thriving midsection, we climb onto the

Conveyor Line, a simple tram-like transport system that connects the major districts and streets around Outer Haven.

Unlike a tram, you don't get to sit down, but merely stand on the conveyor belt and cling onto a pole in front of you as it slides along its tracks. It's not overly fast, but helps you get about much quicker than you would on foot. Using it when tired or intoxicated, however, isn't the best idea. Slipping off at its admittedly low top speed can still cause all manner of physical harm.

Bearing that in mind, I make sure to take the spot behind Tess, weary as she still appears to be. Standing right behind her, I keep a close eye to ensure that she stays steady as the conveyor belt takes us southwards along the central connective street between the west and south quarters.

As we go, the mist begins to clear a little, and the various billboards and advertising displays that dominate the sides of buildings start to spring into life, drenching the world in a multi-coloured neon glow.

To the left, my gaze is drawn to the tall, soaring tower that monopolises the skyline, overshadowing all other structures across the city. Standing up well over a hundred storeys, and circular in shape, the High Tower is the central core of the city, right at the heart of Inner Haven. Up at its glass domed summit, the Consortium, the rulers of the city, cast their eyes down on us from their lofty perch.

Surrounding the High Tower, other grand

buildings spread, sleek and modern and well appointed as far as I can gather - not that I've ever seen them up close. They're all enclosed by a solid metal wall that acts as the boundary between the two parts of the city: Inner and Outer Haven.

Few from Outer Haven ever cross that threshold, our value not deemed high enough to merit doing so. As far as they see it, they're genetically superior to us, and I suppose that's factually correct. To them, we're merely a function of *their* society, a necessary part of the well-oiled machine that they operate.

We're well cared for, and given certain freedoms, and in exchange are expected to play along and stay civil. As far as I see it, the relationship is like that of a man and his dog. The man will treat his dog well, but if it steps out of line, and tries to bite him, he might just put it down.

That is the fine line we all walk down here, looked down on by the members of the 'Enhanced' above us, those with genetically superior traits and abilities. And even within their ranks, there are obvious divisions, those with super intellect rising to the highest class of the Court, and the best amongst those joining the ruling party of the Consortium.

Around here, the mind is everything.

I continue to stare at the High Tower for as long as it stays in view, growing ever clearer as the morning mist fades. By the time we enter the southern quarter, however, some of the taller buildings of Outer Haven serve to block my view.

Down here, the more decadent members of our own class, colloquially known as the 'Unenhanced', tend to live and congregate. Even among our bustling population, social and class divides are obvious.

Here, you have restaurants and marketplaces, art installations and theatre performances. On the other side of Outer Haven, however, in the northern quarter, the Disposables dwell, hidden in their alleys, creeping out at night to pillage and steal.

I suppose I'm somewhere in the middle of that system, occupying the centre ground of our class of Unenhanced. Not quite the bottom rung of the social ladder, but pretty close to it.

Soon enough, the sky is changing colour and the sun is beginning to rise, bringing the warming hues of dawn with it. More people begin to emerge too, spreading out from buildings to get on with their days. As the Conveyor Line slows at certain stops along its path, people step on, taking hold of poles before they're whisked away on their onward journeys.

Before long, it's time for Tess and me to step off. Around us, the vibrant streets of Culture Corner spread, the central hub of art and music in the city. All over, beautiful murals have been painted on walls, and strange sculptures erected from the earth, littered across a wide-open square.

Theatres dot the area too, along with open-air areas used for live performances that are commonly free for the public. It's a whole mess of colour and vibrancy, musicians singing and filling the air with fine music, entertainers busking for change around every nook and cranny.

Yet there's nowhere in the city that's more closely watched either.

Sentry drones hover, and fixed cameras lie hidden in the walls. Those from on high maintain a constant, vigilant eye on the area, making sure that the freedom of expression they continue to grant us doesn't go too far.

Some members of the Enhanced even linger here, sent from Inner Haven to keep a more direct watch. Among them are Brutes, those with superior physical strength, who tend to act as guards and rangers. Hawks, too, creep around among us, their eyesight as sharp as the birds of prey they're locally named after.

Occasionally, the highest class of the Enhanced, Savants, may even find themselves down here, sent on some public relations mission or to try to help decipher a particularly dastardly crime. Savants, you see, are those blessed with superior intellect, and are the ones who make up the Court. And from their most gifted members, the Consortium is chosen.

As I step into the centre of the main square, I search for the vandalism that has drawn us here today. Immediately, the dull black and white writing appears, covering a large and beautifully painted mural depicting mountains and rivers and verdant woods, things that now lie within the toxic wasteland beyond our borders.

The large words, written in block print, merely read:

ART IS EVIL. EMOTION IS EVIL.

GIVE IN TO LOGIC.

To my side, Tess mutters and shakes her head, looking upon the graffiti.

"Fanatics," she mumbles.

I share the sentiment.

One of the natural side-effects of the Savants' supreme intellect is their lacking emotions and devotion to logic. All members of the Court suffer from the same affliction, and that is precisely why it is the Savants who are considered highest among all the Enhanced. The rest – Brutes and Hawks and Dashers, recognised for their astonishing speed – aren't quite so cold and callous in their thinking, yet fall in line just like everyone else. Only, they get to live in Inner Haven, rather than down here with the rest of us.

What's ironic about these Fanatics, however, is that they're not Savants at all.

They're Unenhanced, normal members of the population of Outer Haven, doing regular jobs and propping up those above us just like everyone else.

Yet, during their spare time, they don their black masks and come down here, defacing wonderful pieces of art with their stupid, boring block letters. And that's all despite the fact that the Consortium itself allows us the freedom to express our emotions.

As long as we don't cross the line, that is…

I let out a long, drawn out sigh and shake my head at the irony of it all. Beside the mural, a little collection of people have gathered, all of them looking at the graffiti with a deep measure of displeasure.

We hurry over to join them, and their eyes drop to us.

"Ah, you must be the cleaners," says one man. He looks like a local member of the Council of the Unenhanced, dressed in a rather drab grey suit. I suppose, among our class, they're the highest members, and see to the general day-to-day running of Outer Haven.

"That's us," I say, swinging my bag off my back. "I guess we'll get started?"

I'm rather eager to get this done.

"Um, yes please. If you could remove the graffiti without disturbing the art, we'd all be very grateful. Particularly Humphrey."

My eyes switch to the man to his left, a more colourful character with long brown hair, a pointed chin, and a silly little moustache. His eyes plead with me before his words even come out.

"Please, can you?" he asks in a soft, upset voice.

"Erm, we'll try," says Tess flatly. "But…don't get your hopes up."

I chuckle a little inside at Tess's forward manner. If I didn't know it, I'd guess she had some Savant blood in her herself, given how tactless and unemotional she can be sometimes.

"Well, do your best," says the councilman again. "We have performances across the square later, so we'd love it if you could do a swift job."

"Sure, no problem," I say, before Tess can dish out another one of her barbs.

As they wander off, the artist's eyes dolefully looking upon his tarnished work, Tess raises her eyebrows to me.

"That painting's a goner and you know it," she says. "There's no point in lying to him."

I shrug and open up my bag, scooping out the various tools we'll need for the job. She's right, that's for sure.

Beautiful as it is, this mural's had its day.

We set to work, starting out by scrubbing lightly in a bid to remove the graffiti without completely destroying the art beneath it. When that proves fruitless, we give up the pretence and put a bit more elbow grease into it, the letters only coming off along with the woods and mountains and blue rivers they cover.

"Ah well," says Tess dispassionately, looking upon the mess. "We tried…"

I'm well aware that she has little interest in art and music anyway. Sometimes, when you witness your parents being killed right in front of your eyes, it's hard to take pleasure in much of anything.

Across the square, the artist spends the first hour or two hovering around, yelping any time we finish up on a particular letter, leaving his masterpiece scrambled behind. Soon enough, he disappears entirely, tears spreading down his face as he's led away by a couple of consoling friends.

Clearly, he can't stomach watching his work be scrubbed away so ruthlessly.

Then again, that was his job, and this is ours. Our remit was to remove the graffiti, no quarter given to what it was covering. The order will likely have come from our own council, without the input of the Court. Frankly, why should they care if such a statement is emblazed across the mural of a landscape?

At the end of the day, the words are exactly what they believe. Well, almost. I mean, they wouldn't necessarily call art and emotion 'evil' per se, but they'd certainly agree that is has no tangible impact on the functioning of *their* society.

The Fanatics are aware of this, and clearly agree with it. For them, and the divine 'super-beings' they worship, logic trumps emotion when attempting to rebuild a prosperous civilisation.

And *rebuild* is certainly the word.

The square begins to fill as lunchtime approaches, workers spreading from nearby buildings and offices and warehouses to get a little dose of culture before their days resume. They congregate here from far and wide, the Conveyor Line fit to bursting as it brings in wave after wave of Unenhanced.

Our job still to be completed, we soldier on, and become something of an attraction ourselves. I can hear people whispering around us, trying to figure out what the graffiti would have said with only a few letters still remaining. The brighter among them are quick to work it out.

Frankly, it hardly takes a Savant to do so.

By the time the job is completed, the square is just starting to clear again, the worker bees all called back to their hives. As we pack away our things and prepare to return to the academy, the councilman wanders back over, perusing our work as he comes.

"Good job," he says. "I knew you'd never be able to save the art underneath. Poor old Humphrey, he worked on that piece for weeks. But, needs must I suppose." He digs into his pocket and draws out an envelope. "Payment for your work. Send my regards to Mrs Carmichael."

He wanders off, disappearing into the fading crowd. As he does so, I feel my eye drawn to a black mass spreading from one of its far corners. Four figures, all huddled closely together, begin rushing through towards the centre of the square, all of them dressed entirely in black. They move at such a pace, and so tightly knit together, that they draw many eyes, people stopping and watching as they go.

"What's going on?" asks Tess, following my gaze. "Another stupid performance no doubt…"

I suspect she's right.

The figures continue to come, moving as centrally as they can and drawing along a wave of onlookers in their wake. Anything unusual around here tends to catch the public's attention, the crowd hungrily gobbling up this sort of random performance art.

Personally, it's not usually to my taste, but there's something intriguing about these four. Something that captures my attention as I stand rooted to the spot, watching as they stop in the centre of the square amid the statues and monuments and little audiences that congregate around other entertainers.

Then, suddenly, they spread out, their paths diverging.

Each moves off in an opposite direction, spreading into a wide square, the crowd stepping back to allow them free movement. Behind them, they appear to be dragging something, a transparent sheet, stretching it out across the concrete.

With no warning at all, the four figures stop, and the sheet crackles and flashes, fizzing on the surface of the ground as it sparks into a rhythmic blaze of colourful fire. The people whoop and clap, watching the pretty display.

But something inside me calls out a warning.

This doesn't feel right at all.

The fire crackles for a brief few seconds, and the sheet disappears. As it does so, black markings remain, scorched onto the earth. The throng go silent, all eyes peering closely to read the words.

I don't need to.

I've spent the entire day trying to scrub them out.

ART IS EVIL.

EMOTION IS EVIL.

GIVE IN TO LOGIC.

A confusion breeds in the crowd. People turn to look at the four mystery figures with a new expression: one of anger, and fear.

The black figures stay where they are. For a moment, none of them move.

And then they all move together.

With a coordinated motion, they all reach to their chests, and tear open the loose fabric that binds their black overalls. I squint forward at the nearest man, several dozen metres away, and feel my heart bursting inside my chest at the sight.

Bombs...

Around all their chests, rudimentary explosives are attached. A spread of fear rumbles through the crowd as they all scream and disperse.

But it's too late.

As people scream out, and the crowd flee, the four figures nod to each other in unison.

And with my feet still rooted in place, I watch as the square erupts into a ball of flame.

CHAPTER THREE

It's Tess who reacts the quicker of the two of us.

Grabbing me by the shoulders, she pulls me back and around the side of the mural, tossing me to the floor as she does so. I stumble and fall and feel the heat as she comes down on top of me, the earth rumbling beneath us and the air filling with a deafening roar.

Hidden from the explosion, we huddle in a bundle of limbs on the ground for what seems like minutes. In reality, it's only seconds.

The burst of noise is so loud that it leaves my ears ringing. After the sudden wave of heat comes one of smoke, black and dark grey fumes pouring out from the centre of the square.

For a moment, the aftermath of the explosion leaves a deathly silence in its wake. And then, slowly, the sounds of muffled screams spread into my ears again.

I lock eyes with Tess. Hers are hooded and yet alert, shining blue as the fog of smoke surrounds us.

"Are you OK?" she shouts as me.

I nod, and she stands back to her feet, peering back around the side of the mural. Her mouth slowly falls open as she gawps at the scene. I clamber to my feet, still half dazed, and take a look as well.

Devastation is the only word that springs to mind.

What was once the centre of the square is now a warzone. Little remains but for chunks of statues and monuments too sturdy to be completely eliminated by the blast. Bodies lie everywhere, cut up and torn apart, Culture Corner now coloured in a fresh coating of red blood.

On the outskirts of the blast, the injured cough and try to get to their feet, people spreading in from outside to help. Among them I see some Enhanced rush in, the towering figures of Brutes, dressed in the dark grey and black uniforms of the City Guard, hoisting people into their gigantic arms and getting them to safety.

Perched up on nearby rooftops, Hawks watch on too, their eagle eyes relaying information down to their fellow members of the Enhanced. I watch in awe as a couple of Dashers come hurtling in from nearby, their bodies moving so swiftly through the dispersing cloud of smoke, leaving clear trails behind them. They dart from person to person, checking for pulses and diagnosing injuries at a frightening speed. Determining who can be saved. And who are too far gone.

It's at times like this when you see these people for what they truly are: superior. Remarkable. A higher evolution of the species.

Never have I witnessed them working together with such efficiency.

Quickly, Tess and I add our own bodies to the fray. Right before us, several people who'd caught the fringe of the blast lie clinging onto wounds and wailing to the heavens. As we step in to help them, a Dasher comes whizzing towards us, appearing as if from nowhere.

"No, not this one," he says, his voice rushing as quickly as his feet. It's a common side effect for Enhanced of his kind, talking in abbreviated bursts. "She may have a fractured spine. Don't move her."

"Um, OK," murmurs Tess, looking at the guy with no small measure of wonder.

His eyes quickly dash to a couple of others, moaning nearby and bleeding from lacerations across their legs.

"Help those two," he orders. "Wrap their wounds and halt the flow of blood."

He doesn't offer any further advice. Instead, he calls out loudly for a medic, before performing a closer inspection of the wounded woman at our feet.

Without delay, Tess and I set about helping where we can. Removing our jackets, we peel off our jumpers and begin shredding them to use for bandages and tourniquets, wrapping them tight around wounds as our hands are quickly soaked in blood.

Tess doesn't recoil from the sight at all. It surprises me that the image of torn up legs and spurting blood has no impact on her, given her past. For me, it's unpleasant, but not enough to prevent me from taking action. Together, we wrap the wounds and help to remove the two patients from the battlefield and towards an incoming army of awaiting ambulances.

Before long, a mini field hospital is being erected on the perimeter of the square. More bodies pile in, helping where they can, all the medics in the area called upon. Tess and I continue to offer our aid, working to support more of the injured as they limp and stumble their way towards proper medical treatment.

Everything happens in a bit of a rush, the scent of smoke and seared flesh lingering in the air. It's a smell that puts the odour present back at the academy to shame. One my nostrils have never encountered before.

Truth be told, I never expected to know what charred human bodies smelt like.

It's not until we get a moment to stop and rest that I notice that Tess herself is bleeding from a laceration on her upper right arm. I, too, have a couple of small cuts on my forehead, and a grazed cheek from when I was bundled to the floor.

We move over to the field hospital to get some attention. Tess's arm is hastily sewn up by a medical stapler that pulls the torn flesh together, and then sears the wound shut. My own cuts require nothing but a bit of antiseptic cream, which Tess herself spreads onto my skin.

Standing on the boundary of the square, we both take a long breath and look upon the carnage.

Neither of us speak for a moment as we try to come to terms with what's just happened.

Around us dozens, maybe even hundreds, lie dead or wounded, Culture Corner now a morgue. Never before have the Fanatics committed such an atrocity. Graffiti and vandalism is one thing. This is something else entirely.

As we stand there, a figure stands out amid the rubble and debris in the middle of the square, sweeping in with a couple of armoured Brutes to his sides.

He wears a light grey suit, the sleeves tightly bound around his long arms, the collar buttoned up tight to the top of his neck with his head sprouting from the opening. A neat covering of perfectly manicured brown hair adorns the top of his head, his expression detached and unwelcoming.

There's nothing decorative about his appearance at all, save the small insignia that sits on the middle of his chest below his collar: three circles, one inside the other, each signifying the three main classes of people in the city – the Unenhanced, the Enhanced, and the Court.

The innermost circle is coloured white, indicating that he's a Savant, a member of the Court. The other two circles, representing the Enhanced and us, the Unenhanced, are coloured black.

The Brutes to his flanks carry the same insignia on their armour. Only, with them, the middle circle is white and the other two are black. Often you'll see members of our own Council of the Unenhanced

31

here in Outer Haven with the same badge. With them, of course, it's the outer circle that's white, proof of their more lowly standing.

Overall, it's a quick and easy way to determine what class a particular city servant or official belongs to.

Even without the insignia, however, I'd know this man was a Savant. It's in the eyes, pale blue, showing no emotion at all. His expression, flat and cold, even when looking upon a scene of such devastation, makes it clear that this man has little empathy for what's happened here.

Yet, this sort of attack is unprecedented, and so here he is. Only when something extreme happens do any members of the Court appear, sent down here by the Consortium to ensure that public order is maintained. This man, however, is not from the Consortium from what I can tell. Within the class of the Court, their own hierarchy is determined by the colours of their clothing. Wearing light grey signifies that he's high up, but not at the top of the tree. If he were, he'd be draped in the purest of whites, the blank, colourless attire reserved for those of the Consortium.

Never before has one of their rank come here to Outer Haven. As far as I know, they remain at the summit of the High Tower, and rarely even venture out into the streets of Inner Haven. For them, even meddling with members of the Enhanced is probably deemed an act of impurity. I can't imagine what they'd feel like if they had to endure where I lived for a day or two.

But of course…they don't *feel* at all. How stupid of me.

As I watch the man enter the square, I wonder what type of Savant he is. All Savants have supreme intellect, and all are members of the Court. Yet within their ranks, some rare specimens can be found, those with additional mental abilities that boggle a simple mind such as mine.

I've heard of those who have the power of telekinesis, capable of moving things with nothing but their thoughts. Around here, they're known as Mind-Movers, and exist as little more than rumours heard on the streets and among the youngsters of the academy.

Others apparently have the gift of telepathy, the psychic ability to communicate with each other through their thoughts. I've even heard about them being able to read minds, sneaking into people's heads and seeing their innermost thoughts play out in front of them. We call them Mind-Manipulators.

Given that such powers exist in the mind, there's no way to determine what other gifts a Savant might have purely by looking at them. Brutes are easy to spot for their colossal size and heavy, plodding demeanour. Hawks have intense eyes that glare and rarely blink. Savants – other than the detached and neutral expressions that adorn their faces – have no physical traits that call them apart.

By the look of the man, however, his role is within the City Guard. Most likely one of their senior members, overseeing the various Brutes and Hawks and Dashers who keep watch over the residents of Outer Haven to make sure we stay in line.

Mostly, they tend to do just that – watch – and not take an active part in dealing with most criminal activity. That is the domain of our own police force here, who are tasked with maintaining law and order. When a larger state crime occurs, however, the Enhanced and City Guard will get involved.

Clearly, this is one of those.

I find myself strangely transfixed by the Savant, so rarely are they seen. Tess, too, doesn't utter a word as we just stand there, watching him passing along orders with a cold detachment. From around the square, other members of the City Guard rush over to update him on what's been happening.

One of them, who I recognise as the Dasher who briefly engaged with Tess and me, swiftly darts to his side. As he speaks, his eyes wash over the square, before landing on us. A finger quickly rises up and points us out, and the eyes of the Savant land squarely upon us.

I feel my pulse quicken as I lock eyes with him. Even from this distance, it's like looking into a void, a deep well, emptied out of any emotion or feeling.

With a casual and yet efficient walk, he begins marching in our direction. I share a look with Tess. *Is he coming to talk to us?*

Part of me wants to sink back into the crowd and disappear, but we stand our ground. As he glides in closer, his eyes never leave us. Try as I might to reciprocate, I can't. I find myself looking away, his unblinking eyes making me strangely uncomfortable.

When he arrives in front of us, he stops and attempts to raise a smile on his thin lips. It's all wrong. The shape of his lips and the relentless, disconnected staring of his eyes is completely incongruous. As if the upper and lower parts of his face are reading from entirely different scripts.

An attempt to humanise himself, perhaps, and display some emotion for our own benefit. Frankly, it doesn't work at all. It merely makes him appear even more creepy.

"Good afternoon, ladies. My name is Leyton Burns, Deputy Commander of the City Guard. I am told that you have been aiding us in the clean-up?"

Arg. Clean up. Even his wording is off. He makes it sound like someone's spilled a can of paint or something. Maybe it's all that red blood...

"Yes, Deputy," answers Tess, putting on her 'respectful' voice. "We've been doing what we can."

"And we thank you for it," says Deputy Burns, attempting to lift his smile a little higher. I cringe at the sight. The partial monotone quality to his voice is also rather unnerving. "I am told, too, that you witnessed the explosion?"

"We did," answers Tess.

Deputy Burns nods, staring now directly into Tess's brighter blue eyes. She frowns and recoils a

35

touch.

"Please, don't move," says Deputy Burns. "Stare right into my eyes. This will only take a minute."

I can see Tess struggling to do as she's told. His odd, staring eyes peer deep, his entire body still as a statue. I watch on, unable to look away from the strange scene, as Tess's breathing grows a little more abbreviated. Then, suddenly, Deputy Burns seems to come back to life, leaning back and nodding.

"Good," he says.

Then he turns to me.

"What was that?" I ask, noting the strange expression on Tess's face, as if she's just waking from a dream.

"I searched her hippocampus to trace her memory," he says. "It's the centre of memory and emotion in the brain."

He looks to me, and then seems to remember he's speaking with an Unenhanced. "To put it *simply*," he adds, "I read her mind to see the event for myself from her viewpoint. Now, please be still."

Once more, his eyes seem to lock in place, going completely still as they stare right into mine. I feel like I'm involved in the most intense staring contest ever conceived, something that the kids play back at the academy.

I was never very good at it.

Right now, though, I have no choice. I hold my

hazel irises on his pale blue ones, and try to ignore everything else that's going on around me. Within seconds, my eyes begin to ache, and I feel a strange sense of constriction in my head, as if my brain's being squeezed in a vice.

It's as though I can feel him in my head, poking around and searching for the right memory. It's an invasive and unpleasant act that leaves me feeling a little violated. A person's memory is the most sacred part of them. It's what makes them who they are. No stranger should ever be invited in.

Mercifully, it doesn't last long.

Slowly, the darkness that encloses my vision fades, and the world comes back into view. I look at Deputy Burns, and see the first sign of some expression on his face. A little frown hangs over his eyes, his otherwise pristine forehead ever so slightly wrinkled.

"Tell me. What is your name?" he asks me, a curiosity in his voice.

"Brie Melrose," I say.

"And where do you live, Brie?"

"We both live at Carmichael's Academy," I say. "Her name's Tess Bradbury."

His eyes move to Tess briefly, before coming back to mine.

"I see. Well, I thank you both for your time today. Please, continue with your afternoons. We will take it from here."

He performs a courteous little nod, inspects me for just a second longer, and then turns on his heels and glides off again, accompanied by his two guards.

We watch him go, and for the first time since he approached, I feel myself beginning to breathe normally again.

"That was…weird," says Tess. "I didn't like that at all."

"Nor did I," I say. "I feel like I need a shower."

Tess manages a chuckle, but quickly realises it's completely out of place for this particular situation. Surrounded by corpses, this is hardly the place to be caught laughing. More than anything, though, it's a chuckle of awkwardness. And I know exactly how she feels.

Still standing there, a croaky call sounds behind us.

"Girls! Girls!"

We turn together to see Mrs Carmichael come shuffling along on her old legs, wearing a threadbare old maroon dress and scruffy leather jacket. Her eyes are in stark contrast to those of the Deputy, filled with turmoil and worry as she rushes on.

"Girls, you're OK! Oh thank God. I heard about the explosion…I can't believe it…"

She sweeps us both into her arms, locking us in tight, the stench of tobacco that she carries along with her briefly overpowering the odour of scorched flesh and smoke that continues to linger in the air.

Releasing us, she quickly gazes upon the minor wounds we carry, before inspecting our eyes in a wholly different manner to Deputy Burns. Then, it's to the man himself that her eyes move, turning to him as he continues to coordinate matters on the other side of the square.

"Who was that man?" she asks intently.

"Deputy Commander of the City Guard," says Tess, looking at him once more with an element of fascination.

"A Savant? A member of the Court?" asks Mrs Carmichael quickly.

"That, and more," Tess says. "He was a Mind-Manipulator."

A hint of concern shows in our guardian's eyes.

"He read your minds?" she asks, looking directly at us with a frown.

"Yeah," I say. "He wanted to see what happened from our viewpoint. Nothing major."

"That's all?"

"Yup," remarks Tess. "It was kinda weird. It didn't hurt or anything, it just felt, I don't know, I can't think of the word…"

"Intrusive," I offer.

"Yeah, that's it. Intrusive. Like finding some random person in your bedroom, rooting through your personal stuff."

Mrs Carmichael takes a breath, but continues to

look concerned.

"Is something wrong, Mrs Carmichael?" I ask.

She seems to right herself, pulling her lips up into an awkward smile.

"No, nothing. I'm just…as long as you girls are OK, that's all that matters to me."

She pulls us into another hug, displaying far more affection than normal. Mostly, she's fairly tough, not the type to cry or get emotional about things. It's a symptom of the job, really. Half of those who come to the academy will end up back on the street later in life. Getting too attached to us isn't usually part of the job.

It's clear, however, that those she's known the longest are quite dear to her.

She turns from the scene, seemingly unwilling to spend too long looking at it. Or maybe it's the Deputy who she'd prefer to avoid. Her views on the Enhanced, and the Savants in particular, are fairly well documented around the academy.

"Come now, girls. You've done all you can here. Let's go back home. You can tell me all about it there."

With a rare haste – Mrs Carmichael doesn't tend to do anything quickly these days – she ushers us away from the scene.

Sparing one final glance at Deputy Burns as she goes.

CHAPTER FOUR

That night, Tess and I are the talk of the town.

Well, the academy at least.

Our mere presence down at Culture Corner that morning during the explosion would have been enough to garner plenty of interest from the youngsters. The fact that we actually helped out, and spoke with a Savant – and a Mind-Manipulator at that – is likely the most exciting news to be shared around the occupants of Carmichael's for many a year.

Most of all, however, it's the fact that we actually had our minds read that causes the biggest stir. Around here, the mere existence of Mind-Manipulators and Mind-Movers has always been considered little more than rumour. Now, we have definitive confirmation that such beings are out there, capable of mental feats that are, frankly, frightening.

Sitting in the drab and dreary canteen at dinnertime, we find ourselves being constantly harassed by the ground floor dwellers of the orphanage. At first, we have no problem in telling our tale, recounting the day's events as the children gather round, hanging on our every word.

For the most part, I take the lead – Tess isn't much of a raconteur – giving the kids the essentials of the story without going into too much gory detail. I know that Mrs Carmichael wouldn't want them hearing of such things. And, well, I'd rather not think about them either.

By the time I'm done with the first round, however, several others have gathered, some coming in half way through the story and others appearing right at the end. Naturally, I'm begged to tell it again.

When a second telling turns into a third and fourth, however, I'm beginning to grow weary of it all. Each time, I provide less detail and skip through the events without much enthusiasm. Truth be told, it's not exactly something to be enthusiastic about, seeing so many good, innocent people die.

Yet, there's no denying that it was exciting. Around here, little of note happens, years passing by without any sort of incident to rival what happened out there in Culture Corner. And for these kids in particular, such an event is likely to provide enough fuel for months of gossip and rumour and little re-enactments when it comes to playtime.

The appearance of Mrs Carmichael, however, is enough to douse the flames, her mere presence bringing some semblance of order back into the room.

"Come on now, kids, leave the girls alone. They've been through enough today as it is."

The kids scatter, giggling as they return to their

old wooden tables and benches, tucking back into the gruel that is the most regular feature of our dinnertime diets. Occasionally, if we've had a good week or month, or it's a particularly special occasion – such as a leaving party for one of our senior members after getting granted a housing licence – we will have a more hearty meal.

Some nice soup for starters, perhaps, followed by a bit of proper cooked meat, like chicken, along with potatoes grown over in the agricultural district in the east of town. Then, if we're really lucky, a bit of cake might be passed around. Chocolate is my favourite.

But that's rare. Mostly, it's the processed gruel that we have to endure, tasteless and runny, but containing all the vital nutrients the body needs.

Apparently.

Given the self-sufficient nature of the academy, it's the kids in transition who generally take charge of cooking and serving the food. They plod around, fetching our empty bowls when we're done, some of them sneered at and mocked by the kids beneath them. Soon enough, some of those kids will reach working age. When they can't find work, they won't be sneering anymore.

One of the *transitioners*, however, plods a lot louder than most. As Tess and I quietly discuss the day's events, in private now, the sound of heavy footsteps behind us precedes his presence.

Before he even reaches the table, I know who it is.

We both turn to see his meaty hands reaching out to scoop up our bowls.

"You done?" he asks, his voice like a foghorn.

Tess quickly inspects the remains of her bowl and offers a look of disgust.

"Yeah, Drum, I think we are."

Drum, of course, isn't his real name. His proper given name is Josh, I think. Frankly, it's been so long since I heard anyone call him that that I can't be sure anymore. Even Mrs Carmichael uses his nickname.

It's his gigantic frame, you see. That heavy footfall of his, and the steady pace he tends to keep. Basically, it's like hearing a drum beating as he walks, and you can always hear him coming before he appears.

For a boy of 16, he's simply gigantic. I swear there must be some old Brute blood in him, maybe from a good few generations ago. Surely, somewhere back in his family tree, a Brute got together with a regular Unenhanced, and somewhere down the line, Drum popped out.

Really, he's *that* big.

It wouldn't be too hard to believe, to be honest. Enhanced and Unenhanced have bred for generations, all the way back to when the Enhanced were first created.

Back then, hundreds of years ago, they were simply the result of genetic engineering. Science experiments to create 'superior' beings for the military, humans modified for war. Soldiers and scouts and things like that. It's in their blood, and that's why the Brutes and Hawks and Dashers still primarily work in that same field today.

The creation of Savants was just the next step. Areas of the brain were unlocked, creating people with supreme mental capabilities. From there, the sky seemed to be the limit, the human mind outstripping the pace of the natural evolutionary order, people playing God.

Then, God fought back.

Wars were raged with these new fighting forces. New weapons were constructed by the Savants. Cities were decimated. Biological warfare spread, leaving much of the world uninhabitable and toxic. Across the globe, billions died, and the world began to fall into a growing darkness.

And yet, from the ashes, some remained, and even thrived. The Enhanced, led by the Savants, came together and the city of Haven was born, closeted in an area once known as America across a stretch of land unspoiled by the chaos that tore the world to shreds.

They built the city up into its two component parts, giving Outer Haven to the Unenhanced, and keeping Inner Haven to themselves. A symbiotic relationship was formed. We perform most of the work, and they provide security and protection, keeping us safe from any outside threats.

Truly, they need us as much as we need them, their main goal now to create a prosperous world once more. To clear the toxic wasteland beyond our borders, and rebuild the once great nation we shared.

And it's within that context that their devotion to logic comes to the fore. When the species is under threat, emotion needs to be taken out of the game. As rulers, that is their job, their role. But down here, in the bustling world of Outer Haven, our civil liberties and freedoms are maintained. And while they no longer enjoy such things themselves, they appear to understand that, for us, they're essential elements of life.

I suppose it's necessary for them to humour us in that sense, given what we do contribute. I can't imagine the Savants coming down here and growing the foods they eat, or performing the manual labour that needs doing. They think things up, and we put them into action. That's the division of labour.

Right now, the highest priority among their ranks seems to be clearing the nearby woods and forested regions outside our borders. To the west and south, vast swathes of land lie waiting to be cultivated and used. If, that is, they can be cleared of their toxicity. As it stands, they're making some progress, but it's slow, and much of the land outside of the city remains beyond our reach.

Most striking, perhaps, are the mountains to the northwest. On clear days – of which there are few, owing to the mist that perpetually hovers over the lands – they can be partially visible, grand natural formations way off in the distance.

Only from on high can you really see them, and for me that means hiking over to the eastern quarter, all the way on the other side of the city, where the land rises up a little. From there, the shape of the earth beyond our borders is more visible, something that's always held a strange allure for me. A yearning, perhaps, to find out what's out there.

And then, when my eyes lift up to the High Tower, I feel that pang of jealousy. From up there, they can see far and wide, way over to the mountains and the forests and woods. Maybe even to the coast, far to the east, beyond the swamps and old relics of crushed cities that scatter the earth.

It's just another perk of life as a Savant. One that, ironically, they probably don't even appreciate. Devoid of any deep emotion, I wonder what they feel when they see the towering peaks, and imagine how prosperous the world once was?

Do they feel anything at all? Anything beyond a desire to see our species prosper? They may think they're more evolved, more advanced, but that's not how I look at it.

To me, they're handicapped. To me, they're inhuman.

As far as I see it, advancing the *human* race isn't what they're doing. Because they're not human at all.

CHAPTER FIVE

Before Drum can plod off with our half-eaten bowls of gruel, he lumbers onto the bench in front of us to take a break at our invitation.

For all his physical strength and size, he's rather lacking in the mental side of things. There's a perpetual look of puzzlement on his face, something that's certainly hindering his attempts to find work. Occasionally, he'll perform some basic manual labour jobs – work for which you'd think he'd be ideally suited – but even those are few and far between for someone like him.

As it is, his time at the academy is likely running short. He's been of working age for over a year now, and with work in such short supply, Mrs Carmichael will have little choice but to offer his bed up to someone else soon enough when one of the youngsters comes of age.

It's a sad state, really. Aside from Tess, Drum is my favourite person here. I've known him for years, and from the first day I met him was endeared to his nature – despite his colossal size, he's of a quiet and shy disposition, a gentle giant if ever there was one.

Truth be told, he's like a not-so-little brother to me.

As he lowers himself onto the bench, his deep but quietly spoken voice rumbles from inside his cavernous body.

"Are you OK?" he asks, finding it difficult to make eye contact as the question drops from his plentiful lips.

I can't help but smile at him. Not one of the other inhabitants of this place has asked us how we are, except Mrs Carmichael of course. All of them are far more interested in hearing about what happened, and none have even made reference to the cuts on my forehead, or the bandage wrapped around Tess's upper right arm.

His eyes, however, linger on our war wounds, growing tight with concern as they inspect us.

"We're both fine, Drum," I say. "But thanks for asking."

"Yeah, it's just a scratch," adds Tess, tapping her fingers on her bandage to show that there's no pain at all.

A smile builds up on Drum's face, and his dark brown eyes grow a little brighter.

"Good. I heard the explosion from here," he says. "I didn't know you were down there, though. Was it…scary?"

Now that is a question we've fielded all evening. I haven't yet given a truthful response though, telling the kids that it was more exciting than scary. I guess that's what Mrs Carmichael would prefer me to tell them. She won't want any of the more easily frightened ones having nightmares.

Drum, however, deserves the truth, and before Tess can offer up her usual bravado, I say: "I was scared, yeah. Had we been a few metres closer, we could both be dead."

Tess nods to my side. Drum's eyes crinkle up a little tighter.

"But it's all OK now," I make sure to add. "I'm sure it won't happen again."

"You really think so?" asks Drum. "Was it the Fanatics?"

"Yup," says Tess. "But security's going to be much tighter now. The Consortium will no doubt send more Enhanced down, more of the City Guard. More damn eyes on us."

"That's a good thing though, Tess. More Hawks, in particular, to keep an eye on things," I say.

"Good and bad. We don't exactly want loads of Enhanced wandering around do we? These are our streets, not theirs."

I shrug. "As long as it makes the people more safe, I'm on board. At least temporarily."

As we speak, Mrs Carmichael's craggy old voice barks from across the room.

"Drum, break's over now. Come on, there's clearing up that needs doing."

Drum nods subserviently. "Yes, Mrs Carmichael. Sorry, Mrs Carmichael."

I don't think I've ever met anyone as polite as he is.

He rumbles to his feet and moves off, continuing to fetch more empty and half-eaten bowls. His hands and arms are so big he can accommodate many more than anyone else. If he wasn't so large, finding work collecting plates in a restaurant might be easy. Unfortunately, his size makes him clumsy. I've lost count of the number of things he's broken around here.

Mrs Carmichael watches him closely as he gets to the point of overloading his arms.

"Careful now, Drum. If you drop those, you pay for them."

"Yes, Mrs Carmichael," he says again, before plodding off into the kitchen.

"I'm not sure he's long for this place," says Tess, shaking her head as we watch him go. "I know Brenda has a soft spot for him, but she can't give him special treatment."

Tess, unlike me, will occasionally use Mrs Carmichael's first name, depending on the circumstances.

I watch on wistfully, knowing she's right. I doubt how long he'll survive out there on his own. His size could make him a target. A lot of people have an intense dislike for the Enhanced, and a kid as big as Drum will only draw attention.

As he disappears, Mrs Carmichael comes trotting over.

"You must be tired, girls. I suggest you go and get some sleep."

"I'm happy to help clear up," I say.

"No need for that, Brie. You've been through plenty today, and deserve a break. I've made sure that your work tomorrow has been passed onto someone else."

"You mean, we get a day off?" asks Tess excitedly.

"You've earned it. Just relax, and hang out here at the academy."

She breezes away, gathering up the youngsters in a bid to send them off to their dorms. Unlike us, they stay in groups of 6, squashed into tighter quarters. It's a good way of getting more of them off the streets, but sure does lead to some raucous behaviour.

Tonight, I suspect, they'll be discussing the events down at Culture Corner long into the early hours. It's something not even Mrs Carmichael can police.

As she struggles to round them all up, Tess and I begin making our way upstairs to wash and get to bed. Physically, I feel exhausted, and yet mentally there's a freshness that I'd rather wasn't there. Any time a period of quiet dawns, my mind is once more filled with the sounds of screams and the sight of blood and the smell of charred flesh and suffocating smoke.

Most of all, however, it's the strange feeling of having another person inside my head that lingers the most. The sense that my private thoughts, something that no one should ever have access to, have been violated and inspected.

I'm sure that Deputy Burns merely looked for my memory of the attack. Nothing else would be of interest to him. But still, it leaves an unpleasant taste in my mouth that I know a good night's sleep won't be sufficient to eliminate.

Upstairs, Tess and I take it in turns to use the basic shower. It's shared between all those on the top floor, barring Mrs Carmichael, and for the most part has a limited supply of hot water.

Most evenings it's a fight to get there first and make use of the warm water while it lasts. Tonight, Tess and I are given first dibs.

"I could get used to treatment like this," remarks Tess as she comes out, draped in a towel, her skin pink and glowing from the heat.

I quickly take my turn, and enjoy the somewhat rare sensation of warm water trickling down my spine. After only a few short minutes, however, normality resumes and the water goes tepid, calling an end to my brief period of bliss.

Back in our room, I find Tess already tucked up in bed. Her eyes, though, remain wide open as I brush my teeth and drag my nightclothes over my skin, before hopping into bed.

Clearly, her mind is just as busy as mine.

"So, what do you want to do tomorrow?" she asks.

The first thing that comes to mind is: "Sleep."

"Yeah," she laughs. "I could sleep for days I reckon."

"Same here," I say.

We're both lying.

Because as the lights go off, and we try to fall asleep, I know we'll both find it hard. Tess, usually a light snorer – or heavy breather, according to her – makes it very clear when she's sleeping. For several hours that night, locked in the darkness, I don't hear a peep from her.

I lie up against the wall, keeping my glowstick beneath my blanket to douse its light, and stare at my parent's fading faces. I run through the usual routine that I have to perform before dropping off, which mostly sends me into the land of nod with cracked images of my long gone parents in my head.

And of other things, of another life I might have led, a whole world of possibilities where my imagination can run wild.

It's a symptom of life for any orphan, especially those like me who know nothing of where they came from. A chance to escape reality, if only for a while, and live in the imagined world created by your subconscious.

For some, it's the only way to get through the day…just waiting for the night.

Yet that night, my mind doesn't conjure false images of some imagined reality. It doesn't spend its time considering what my life might have been like had I grown up in a more conventional family.

No. That night, it's the sights and smells and sounds of the attack at Culture Corner that dominate. Each time I drop off, they swarm all over me, causing me to wake at regular intervals with my body drenched in a cold sweat.

And while the youngsters down below might be excited by such an event, being there was a very different experience. One that, right now, I'd rather forget.

CHAPTER SIX

The morning brings with it a chill that's more bitter than any I've felt in a while. Peeling off my blanket and sodden nightclothes, I'm quick to dress in my warmest winter attire, before sitting back down on the bed.

A few minutes later, Tess stirs, breaking from a sleep that was probably just as troubled as mine.

"What time is it?" she coughs, shivering underneath her covers.

I scoop up my old watch from the bedside table.

"7.30," I say.

"Arg...why does my stupid body wake me up so early."

"Habit," I mutter, as she rolls over and tries to get some more sleep.

I don't do the same. Frankly, I'm happy to be up, and would rather not give myself over to my subconscious again, keen as it seems to be to torment me with the carnage from yesterday.

Damn subconscious...

Instead, I leave Tess to her rare lie-in, and head downstairs for breakfast to find Drum hard at work in the kitchen, utilising his mighty strength as he stirs a giant pot of porridge. This week it's his turn to prepare breakfast each morning.

"Need some help?" I ask him breezily.

He seems surprised to find me down there. Recently, I've been starting work too early to make breakfast, and have been dining out on those tasteless protein bars instead.

The porridge isn't any better, but at least it's warm.

"Hey Brie," he says, showing off his ginormous gnashers through a smile he reserves for me. "You should rest. This is my job. But thanks for asking."

"Really, Drum, I don't mind. I'll serve. How about that?"

After a brief bit of haggling he agrees, and I begin ladling portions of porridge into bowls. As I do, the noise outside in the canteen begins to grow as the kids come pouring in with an excessive amount of energy.

It's obvious they're even more excited and talkative than usual.

As Drum scoops up a few bowls to serve, I tell him to stay and that I'll handle it. I know he gets teased by the kids, and when they're in this sort of mood, they're only going to be more irritating.

As I emerge from the kitchen, however, I realise that perhaps I haven't thought this through. Immediately, I'm harassed again for further retellings of the previous day's events, something

I'm completely unwilling to relive.

This time I'm not so polite. I tell them in no uncertain terms that they've heard all they're going to hear from me on the matter.

Thankfully, I hold just enough authority around here to calm them, only one or two throwing lacklustre obscenities my way for my trouble. I eye up a particularly difficult child, Brandon, who's usually the chief stirrer among the louder boys, as a couple of swear words drip off his youthful, 13 year old lips.

"I heard that, Brandon," I say, glaring at him. "Don't make me tell Mrs Carmichael on you."

That's enough to shut him up. Mrs Carmichael has a strange aversion to swearing, especially among the younger members here. The younger they are, the worse her reaction.

It's ironic, really, because she's not short of the odd curse word herself. Especially after a glass or two of whiskey.

I try to keep busy that morning. Once breakfast is all over, I help Drum with the washing up, and we chat a little about his working prospects.

"I heard they need more workers on the *outside*," he says. "You know, clearing the woods…"

"Drum, no way are you doing that!" I say. "You know why they need more workers for that?"

He shrugs.

"Because workers *die* all the time," I say. "It's

dangerous out there, you know that."

Work outside of the borders of Outer Haven is notoriously dangerous, and mostly considered a last resort for those in desperate need of money or rations. Generally, it involves clearing the toxic woods and lands beyond our borders, labour that the Unenhanced see to. Monitored, of course, by the Enhanced.

Even inside protective suits, people regularly get sick and end up dying from the suffocating toxic fog. And that's not all they need to worry about. Outside of the city, other threats linger too...

It's upsetting that Drum's even considering it.

"Promise me you won't go down there and sign up," I tell him. "We'll find something better for you. And you've always got Tess and me. You know that, right?"

He nods.

"Say the words, Drum."

"I promise," he mutters.

I step in and give him a short hug, failing as usual to wrap my arms around his gigantic trunk.

As I return to my room later than morning to take my pills, I make a note to talk to Mrs Carmichael about Drum.

Again.

Unfortunately, it's a conversation I've had with her many times before. Try as she might, she's found it hard getting him any sort of regular work.

His size, clumsiness, and general simple-mindedness make him unappealing to most employers.

Back in the room, Tess appears to have roused herself. Looking fresh, and dressed up warm, her eyes sparkle with the promise of having the remainder of the day off.

"Let's go out," she says.

"Mrs Carmichael said we should hang out here," I counter.

"Screw that. I wanna go back down to Culture Corner, see what's going on down there."

"You want to go *back*?" I ask, quite surprised to hear it.

"Yeah, sure. There's not much else to do is there?"

She's got a point. The entertainment around here is sorely lacking, and what there is will almost certainly be occupied by the increasingly annoying youngsters.

Just thinking about their incessant pestering is enough to get me to agree.

"Fine, I guess we could go," I concede. "I'll go check with Mrs…"

"Forget it, Brie. Don't disturb her. We're 18, and can go where we want."

She rushes towards me, grabs my arm, and drags me straight out into the corridor. Before I know it, we're moving out of the building and onto the street, the world rushing with an endless stream of activity outside.

It's a clear day, which is quite rare, clear enough perhaps to get a good view of the western mountains from the higher ground of the eastern quarter. I ask Tess about going there instead, but she has less interest than me in the view, or in imagining what it must be like hiking up in the mountain valleys and passes.

Even the rumours about the mountain dwellers don't seem to interest her.

"Nonsense, that's all it is," she says. "Those mountains are dead and empty."

Tess can be quite the downer when she wants to be. She finds joy in so few things.

I don't argue, but instead make a mental plan to head eastwards later that afternoon, with or without her. Truth be told, without might be better. Looking upon those mountains is something I like to do alone.

As we make our way towards the Conveyor Line, I make note of the increased presence of the City Guard around the streets. Up on the tops of buildings, hidden behind neon signs and transparent holograms, Hawks sit and spy on the world below. At larger intersections, heavyset Brutes stand primed for action, and Dashers await their orders, finding it hard to stay still for too long.

Seeing such a collection of Enhanced, of course, has an impact upon the population, who eye them with a mix of suspicion and awe. There's a wariness about the place, a strange energy. It seems as though people are walking more rigidly than normal, talking in quieter tones.

At times like this, our collective behaviour needs to be impeccable. And we all know it.

Seeing sentry and security drones isn't so uncommon around these parts. And yet still, their own numbers have burgeoned and swelled, the sky almost as busy as the streets for sheer numbers of flying contraptions.

As we reach a larger intersection, huge screens, usually filled with advertising, fill instead with news of the bombing. Video footage of the attack is played, provided by cameras hidden within high buildings and on drones, that give us a whole new perspective of it all.

We stop for a moment and watch, and in the bottom left corner of the screen see ourselves. Standing beside the mural, I see Tess grab my shoulder and fling me to the floor, just as the wall of fire spreads to where we were standing.

"Jesus," I whisper. "I didn't realise we were so close. You saved my life, Tess…"

She shrugs. "Think nothing of it. Just instinct."

The scene continues to play out, and the flames disappear as quickly as they spread, followed by the rush of dark grey smoke. It all seems to happen so much faster watching it, rather than being there.

As Tess and I creep around the side of the mural

again, and look upon the devastation, the camera appears to zoom in on us. It follows us as we stand for a split second, and then dart straight into the fray, quickly moving in to help. Then, the Dasher bursts as if from nowhere, issues his orders, and we're seen tearing apart our jumpers and tending to wounds.

At the bottom of the screen, a headline reads:

Heroes of Outer Haven Save Lives...

We look at each other in astonishment, before the camera angle changes, focusing on another brave soul who ran straight in to help.

"Jeez...we're famous!" laughs Tess.

I don't much like the idea of it. Thankfully, the camera angle was from above us, and our faces were largely obscured by the smoke and mist.

Around us, plenty of other people are watching the screens. None of them, however, lend us a look. It's enough to satisfy me that we shall remain nothing but anonymous heroes.

Then again, I don't see myself as a hero at all. Tess, maybe, for saving my life.

But not me.

We don't linger too long watching the giant screens, and quickly jump aboard the Conveyor Line towards Culture Corner. As we near, it's obvious that the entire area has been cordoned off, the line ending prematurely and not venturing towards the main square as it usually would.

We step off and continue on foot, working our way through the bustling crowd. Soon enough, we've come to the end of the line, unable to move beyond a fence that's been erected on the boundary of the square, guarded by our own police force from Outer Haven, known locally as Con-Cops.

Rumour has it, they're made up of criminals who have been 'reconditioned' by special therapies. Exactly what this means, no one seems to know. But suffice to say, when these criminals go away, they come back as very different people, most of them turning into very loyal and efficient policemen.

It's an effective method, I guess, of utilising those who have done wrong. They'd otherwise be eliminated, depending on the severity of their crimes, or sent for some other term of unpaid manual labour elsewhere. Those deemed appropriate for a life of service are instead made into Con-Cops, swapping a life of crime for one of protection.

Here in Outer Haven, however, criminals are not treated with much leniency. Anyone caught causing any sort of public infraction can easily find their life changing, or even ending, overnight. The Court have no tolerance for such things.

I suppose that comes with the territory when you're cursed with total emotional detachment.

It makes sense, then, that everyone is acting particularly carefully now, with the streets so filled with City Guards and Con-Cops. Even pushing and shoving to the front of the queue to get a good look into the square, as Tess and I are doing now, might not be the best idea.

We do it nonetheless, and quickly realise that there isn't much to see. The place has been swiftly cleaned up, all remains of bodies and old statues now having been removed, and the blood and dust washed away from the concrete floor.

On the outskirts of the square, however, other venues are still being cleaned. Theatres and other works of art remain dusty and blackened, their owners working to clean them up as they once were. I suspect that, for the time being at least, Culture Corner will remain rather quiet.

Still, the investigation appears to be ongoing. As we look forward, various officials appear in conversation. Tess taps me on the arm and draws my attention to one in particular.

"Hey, check it out…it's our friend Deputy Burns."

Amid the rabble, the Deputy appears, dressed exactly as he was yesterday and coolly managing the show. He appears to be addressing a group made up of members of the Council of the Unenhanced, as well as artists and venue owners most affected by the Fanatics' crazed attack.

Among them, I see Humphrey. I doubt the desecration of his beloved mural seems so bad now, given that the entire square lies in ruin.

As I look at the Deputy, I feel the urge to sink away into the crowd again and disappear, my head starting to throb at the sight of him. I begin pressing back, and as I do so step on someone's foot behind me. They yelp out loudly, and push me in the back.

"Watch where you're going will you!"

I turn to see an aggressive looking woman glaring right at me, a redness around her eyes. I immediately wonder if she knew someone who died here yesterday, a thought that quells any desire to retaliate.

The stern voice of a Con-Cop behind the barrier provides another compelling reason.

"Hold up there, what's the problem?" he asks firmly.

"Nothing…nothing," I say. "Just an accident."

The woman's eyes redden further, narrowing.

"First you barge past me, then you stamp on my foot," she cries. "I've been through enough as it is…"

She begins whimpering, confirming my suspicion.

Perhaps barging to the front wasn't such a good idea.

"I'm sorry," I say. "I didn't mean anything by it."

The Con-Cop steps in closer, drawing out an *immobiliser,* a simple baton they all carry with them. Its end begins buzzing menacingly, and he points it straight at me. One little tap with that, anywhere on my body, and I'll go completely rigid, paralysed for a good few minutes.

Depending on what setting it's on, it could be longer.

"You'll keep calm, or I'll take you both in," shouts the Con-Cop, close enough now to zap us both.

Next to me, Tess tries to act mediator. It's not a part she usually plays.

"It's all OK, officer. Really, we're all OK, right ladies?"

She turns to me, and the other woman, with glaring eyes. If she doesn't shut the hell up soon, they'll be hell to pay for us both.

Clearly maddened by grief, however, the woman's having none of it, her cries and accusations only growing louder.

"Shut up!" I mouth to her. "Shut up!"

She doesn't.

"One more peep out of you, and you're getting stung!" shouts the Con-Cop right at her.

She doesn't seem to listen, tears starting to flow freely down her cheeks. The man doesn't take any notice whatsoever in her distress, stepping closer now and preparing to strike.

I look to the poor woman, and feel a surge of sympathy that compels me to act. As the guard's arm coils up, I make my move, reaching out just as he's about to strike and clutching at his wrist to hold him back.

"Don't," I shout at him. "She doesn't deserve it! She's just grieving!"

Behind me, I can feel Tess grabbing me, trying to

pull me away.

"Brie! What the hell are you doing!" she grunts.

Unfortunately, it's too late. I've acted now, and there's no taking that back.

Oh crap...what have I done.

I look into the Con-Cop's eyes, and see a menacing but cold stare. Like the Savants, there's a look of detachment there, one that's led to rumours that the therapies they go through are designed to suppress their emotions and make them more compliant.

With a sudden thrust, however, he pulls his immobiliser away.

"You've done it now, girl," he growls.

I can't move, stuck in among the now chattering crowd as I am. I watch as the man lines me up, and prepares to strike. And just as he does, a call comes from behind him.

"Hold on right there."

The voice is deep, precise and cool. It flows across from the square, and my eyes immediately rise up to see the lean figure of Deputy Burns come easing towards us, wrapped in his light grey suit and flanked by his towering guard of Brutes.

"Officer, stand down. I know these girls," comes his voice.

The Con-Cop's reaction is immediate. In one swift motion, the immobiliser shuts off and he swings it back to his belt, before taking a step back and standing as still as a statue.

Deputy Burns speaks again as he nears, stopping a good way away so as not to get too close to the crowd of Unenhanced.

How horrible it must be for him.

"Officer, let them through."

The guard acts immediately, moving aside the barrier. Tess and I share a look, and step through. We're been spared, saved by the bell.

Unfortunately, it's not a bell I want to hear rung.

CHAPTER SEVEN

"Well, well," says Deputy Burns, once more attempting to bring that odd smile to his face. "Brie Melrose and Tess Bradbury. What a surprise to find you both here."

"Good afternoon, Deputy," I say. "Sorry for causing a scene. It was a misunderstanding."

"Oh, I trust that it was," he says. "Come on over here, girls. I have something to speak with you about."

We share a look. Tess's eyebrows dip into a little frown, and mine do the same.

He's not going to get in our heads again is he?

We move over towards him, and he hastily begins walking off to one side, away from the rabble of watching eyes. As always, his gigantic Brutes walk with him, holding their pace a little way behind at his order. They look alert, a constant vigilance in their narrow eyes.

"It's funny that you came here," continues Deputy Burns. "It saves me having to send a postal drone to Carmichael's. I suppose you could say it's nicer to tell you this in person too."

Again, Tess and I glance at each other, wondering

what he's talking about. We wait for him to continue to get clarification.

"Now, you're aware that a small number of your population performed admirably yesterday immediately after the attack, yes?" he asks, stopping and rounding on us in a quieter part of the square.

We nod.

"We just saw some footage," says Tess.

"Footage of you?" he asks.

"Yes, Deputy. They called us heroes."

"Ah, and I suppose you are. Your kind like to lift people up onto their shoulders during difficult times. They like to feel inspired. The Court understands this, and have decided to honour you."

"Honour us?" I say.

"Yes. We will be holding a ceremony for those who aided us in the clean up."

Arg. Clean up. There's that phrase again.

"You two, along with several others, acted valiantly and bravely. These are traits that interest us, virtues that we believe are important. For an Unenhanced to act as such, with the burden of fear to deal with, is something we respect. And so we will provide you with a rare honour, the opportunity to come to Inner Haven, where the ceremony will be held."

"Inner Haven!" squawks Tess.

Deputy Burns barely reacts to her sudden

excitement. He merely stares at her with his usual bland expression, before nodding.

"Yes. Does that sound good to you both?"

"Erm, yeah!" says Tess, usually so placid herself. A visit to Inner Haven, however, is such a rarity that anyone would likely be enthused by the idea.

"And you, Brie?"

"Yes, Deputy," I answer, maintaining my cool. "Will it take place in the High Tower?"

My thoughts turn to the mountains again. From anywhere near the summit of the High Tower, that view beyond the borders of the city must be magnificent. Something I've yearned to see my entire life.

The Deputy's words, however, speedily douse my flames.

"No, Brie. The ceremony will take place at the base of the High Tower, not within it." He inspects me for a second, and I get the sense he's looking into my mind again, uninvited this time. "You're disappointed," he remarks.

"No, no," I say quickly. "I'm honoured, sir, truly. I've just always wanted to see the view from up there, see the world."

"And why is that?" he asks.

He doesn't get it. That much is clear.

"Curiosity, I guess," I tell him. "I've heard you can see for miles across the mountains and forests, and even to the eastern coast from right at the top."

"That much is true, Brie. I wonder who your source is, though, on this information. Not even I have ever been right to the summit of the High Tower. Only members of the Consortium are invited inside."

"Just rumours," I say. "Speculation, maybe."

"Right. Well, it appears that you're both excited by the idea, given your expressions and your heart-rates."

Jesus...can he sense our heart rates?

"Yes, sir, very excited," says Tess.

"Good," he says, laying his eyes over our bodies, dressed in what he'd probably term 'rags'. "I assume, given your current attire and standing here in Outer Haven, that you have no suitable clothing for a visit to Inner Haven."

He doesn't mince words. Being forward and rude is just another side effect of lacking emotions.

"What's suitable clothing?" asks Tess.

"Not anything you'll see around here," he says. "I'll have someone sent to you to aid you in this matter. Remember, girls, this is an opportunity. I understand you're both currently unattached?"

"Unattached?" I ask.

"Yes. Unmarried. Unpaired. Not betrothed to anyone?"

We look at each other and can't help but laugh. Neither of us have had much luck on that front. Living at Carmichael's, finding a husband hasn't exactly been top of our agenda.

"I suspect your laughter means 'no'," he says.

We shake our heads.

"Well then, consider this an opportunity to impress," he says. "I will send a liaison over to you tomorrow morning to take you through things. The ceremony will be the following day. Good afternoon, girls."

With a rather abrupt finish to the conversation, he turns on his heels and moves back towards the centre of the square, flanked once again by his gargantuan guards.

Tess looks at me, and with a light in her blue eyes says: "We're going to Inner Haven!"

I've never seen her so animated. It's oddly jarring, particularly given her occasional distaste and distrust of the Enhanced. Then again, even those who hate them would find the lure of Inner Haven a fairly attractive prospect, if only to see what life is like there.

Buoyed by the news, we spend the rest of the afternoon over in the eastern quarter, navigating there by way of the Conveyor Line and walking through the large agricultural and food packing districts that dominate the area.

Here, almost all of the food production for the city is managed. Within large warehouses, vegetables and fruits are grown and harvested, and herds of animals are bred and processed into meat. Chickens, cows, pigs, sheep, and various other types of animals are farmed, their lives short and unpleasant.

With space at a premium, they're packed in tight, fed and fattened before being slaughtered. I've always considered it completely inhumane, and never like getting too close to the slaughterhouses where living, breathing animals are so cruelly treated.

Maybe I'm just soft. No one else seems to care.

Tess is among them.

"They're just animals, Brie," she says as I bring up the subject. "Who cares how they feel. They're bred to be eaten."

"If you saw it, you might agree," I say.

I go on to tell her a story of how I had a job here once that involved cleaning out one of the slaughterhouses after a particularly busy day of killing. The amount of blood and gore was enough to put anyone off, but it was the look in the animals' eyes that was the worst.

Kept in a separate room, I wandered in during a break and saw them all, locked up so tight together in pens they could barely move.

"When you see their eyes, you realise they're flesh and blood creatures," I say. "They should be treated better."

Tess still isn't convinced.

"People need to eat, Brie. If a few animals have to suffer, so be it. When we clean the world and make it habitable again, then they can run free. Right now, it's us who need to survive, not them."

Survival. That's the key word. And when survival's at stake, people will do terrible things. And it's not just the Savants either, it's all of us. Those factories are run by normal people, people with emotion. And not one of them seems to batter an eyelid.

Unfortunately, in order to reach the highest ground of Outer Haven, we need to pass through the food district. With Tess unlikely to agree with me, I give up the subject, and lead her towards the summit of an old warehouse in the northeast of the quarter.

At the back, there's a gap in an old fence that surrounds the building. Through we go, and towards a ladder fixed to the rear of the warehouse, taking us right up to the roof.

"So this is where you go," remarks Tess as we reach the top.

It's only a few storeys up, but there's no better place in Outer Haven to look upon the view. From up here, much of the city is visible, from the wall dissecting the two parts of the city, to the wall on its periphery, built to protect us and littered with outposts that keep an eye on the world outside.

Then, beyond those, the natural world comes into view. Only on clear days like this can much be seen, the woods and forests and marshlands to the east and south, and the hills and mountains that climb to the northwest.

"You picked a good day to come up here," I tell

Tess. "It's never this clear."

She stays silent, slowly surveying the scene. I smile as I look upon the wonder in her eyes.

"I get it now," she whispers. "It's kinda...beautiful, isn't it."

"Sure is. There's a whole world out there. A vast, endless one."

We sit for a little while up on the roof, talking about the world beyond. I can't help but feel somewhat vindicated by my decision to come up here. For a while, Tess has shown little interest in seeing the world beyond our borders, knowing she'll never get to see it.

"No point in knowing what's outside when you live inside," is her usual line.

I suspect, after today, her interest in such things might grow.

We stay there until the sun begins to set, drawing a gloomy blanket over the forests and mountains until they disappear entirely. As is often the case, the cooling of the sun and sky brings a mist along with it, descending from the heavens and hanging over the earth.

It's our cue to leave, so we quickly descend from the roof and work our way back towards the nearest boarding point along the Conveyor Line. From there, the quickest way back is probably around the northern side of the city, passing through the north quarter.

Right now, before the light fades completely, it

remains relatively safe. Mostly, it's a residential part of town for the poor folk among us, with an old industrial district at its most northerly point that's long been underutilised. When the world turns dark, however, it can be less than hospitable, and not somewhere to linger for too long.

Thankfully, the Conveyor Line passes straight through it at its southern point, and doesn't venture north where it's more dangerous. Moving around the circumference of Outer Haven, we're soon back in the western quarter and navigating our way down the tighter, narrower streets where we live.

By the time we step through the doors of Carmichael's Academy, we're greeted with even more fanfare than yesterday. By the sounds of the chattering from the youngsters, the footage from the attack has been seen. And unlike the general public, the kids were quick to recognise our part in it.

"You were awesome!" shouts one girl, Abby, looking up at us with wonder and amazement. "I wanna be just like you when I grow up."

Tess laughs and pats her on the head.

"Good choice, kiddo," she says. "Who better than us to emulate!"

Abby doesn't quite cotton onto her sarcasm, and merely beams as she's patted like a dog.

Another boy, Nate, usually so quiet, appears more animated than I've ever seen him. He bustles through to the front and grabs my hand.

"I touched the hero's hand!" he shouts, bringing

whoops and calls from his little posse of friends.

Clearly, it's the younger ones who are most excited by it all. Those who have entered their teens aren't quite so interested, standing back and trying to remain stoic as they watch on. Among them, the head bully, Brandon, sneers and shakes his head, apparently unimpressed.

As a few other kids begin re-enacting our role in the attack, we start pushing through towards the stairs. They hold us back, though, and put on the little show. Evidently it's for our benefit.

For the next few minutes, we're forced to politely endure their re-enactment, pulling all the right faces and trying to appear impressed. Only when Mrs Carmichael's voice filters from the floors above does the show come to an end.

"Brie. Tess. Come up here please, I need to talk to you."

Thank God for that. Saved by the bell again.

With a few disappointed boos from the crowd of ground floor dwellers, we make our way upstairs and towards our patron's quarters. There, we find her behind her desk with her usual glass of whiskey and cigarette on the go. The look of her ashtray suggests she's been getting through a few more than usual.

"Drink?" she asks as we sit down in front of her.

She never invites us to drink...

I decline. Tess accepts. It doesn't surprise me.

The offer of a cigarette, meanwhile, is declined by both. Tess takes a sip of her whiskey and coughs. I look at her like the amateur she is and she retorts with a glare. Our little face-off is broken by Mrs Carmichael's husky voice.

"I had a message today," she begins. "I'm told you've both been invited to Inner Haven."

We both look right at her and nod.

"We saw Deputy Burns again," coughs Tess. "He says there's a ceremony to honour us. How cool is that?"

"Yes, well…firstly, I'm going to ignore the fact that you went out without my consent. I did suggest that you stay here today. I'm not sure returning to Culture Corner was a good idea."

We dip our heads in apology.

"But," she continues, "you'd have gotten the message anyway. At least the Court saw fit to tell me about it first. Apparently they do have *some* manners."

"Who came?" I ask.

"No one. Just a postal drone with a message, stamped with the seal of the Court. They're clearly aware that we have no interface here for video and holographic communication. And that's to say nothing about the fact that they know where you two live…"

"Oh yeah," I mumble. "I told Deputy Burns yesterday. He asked, I couldn't have said nothing."

"Yes, I understand that. It's just unfortunate. I don't want this place coming under any scrutiny. Their thoughts on orphans are quite clear, as you well know."

I am aware. The Court have little interest in charity for the most part. If someone isn't able to offer value in some way or another to society, they're deemed pointless. Occasionally, they'll send out teams to trawl the northern quarter for Disposables if they become too much of a nuisance. When they're caught, they're never seen again.

"Honestly, I don't particularly like the idea of you two going there," she adds. "It's just another public relations device. You're being used as pawns in a game, and it's not on."

"Well, that's a negative way of looking at it, Brenda," says Tess.

I gulp. Perhaps now isn't the time to use her first name. That whiskey is clearly giving her courage.

"I actually feel quite proud and privileged," she continues. "Not many are invited in…"

"Yes, exactly. Not many are, because not many are considered *worthy*. We're people just like they are, my dear, and yet they look down upon us as little more than animals. And why? Superior intellect? Superior physical abilities and senses. None of that has anything to do with being human."

I fear she might go off on one of her rants. From time to time, she'll let off some steam by rambling on against the 'terrible doctrine' of the Consortium, letting out a few of those swear words she doesn't like to hear anyone else use in the process.

These days, I've learned to tune most of it out. And it's almost always after she's had one too many whiskeys.

Today, though, her eyes remain clear and her words aren't slurring one bit. She really means this one.

"It sounds like you don't want us to go?" I ask calmly.

Her eyes come to mine, and stare at me for a moment. I see the lightest shaking of her head, then a whisper drifts from her mouth.

"I don't…"

She scoops up another cigarette and lights up. After a fresh gulp of whiskey she reacquires her composure and speaks again.

"But you will go," she says, a vibe of deflation in her voice. "If *they* want you to go, there's nothing I can do to stop it. Just…make sure you're careful with what you say. And what you think."

Those words call an end to the meeting. We're dismissed, and return to our room, before going down to catch the end of dinner once the youngsters have finished up.

And finding Drum there, the three of us enjoy a quiet dinner, free from harassment and chattering children.

It won't last long.

As soon as we've been to Inner Haven, they'll have a hell of a lot more questions for us.

I guess I'd better enjoy this quiet time while I can.

CHAPTER EIGHT

The following morning, Tess and I wait anxiously for the arrival of Deputy Burns's liaison. Given the company he keeps, we expect a boring old Savant to come wandering through the door. I can't imagine a worse person to spend the morning with.

When the door knocks, however, and we open it up wide, we're surprised to see a beautiful young woman appear before us, perhaps only in her early twenties. I immediately scan the look in her eyes, and inspect the smile on her face, and conclude that the emotion in her expression is real.

"Good morning," she says, her voice velvety and sweet. "My name is Sophie Winchester. You must be Brie and Tess. Now, don't tell me, you're Brie, and you're Tess…"

She looks at me first, and then to my best friend.

"That's right," says Tess.

Sophie beams. "I was told that Brie had hair like mine," she says.

I look at hers, beautifully cut and styled in long brown waves, and shining under the light above, and consider the comparison completely unfavourable. For her, that is.

Sure, my hair is the same colour, or thereabouts. But that's about where the similarities end.

I tell her as much, and she simply says cryptically: "Well, we'll see how it turns out later."

Stepping into the reception hall of the academy, I see her nose crinkle at the smell and her eyes dart about the place with a measure of pity. I feel the urge to apologise for the stench. This woman appears to be very well kept.

Adorning her slender body, a dress of light blue hangs, on top of which is a fashionable jacket of identical colour. I suspect she must be fairly cold, dressed so sparsely, but she offers no sign that she is.

"So, this is where you live?" she asks, looking back to us.

"Yup," says Tess, a little bluntly. "This is home."

"It's, um," says Sophie, clearly trying to find something nice to say. "Well, um, it's..."

"A dump," says Tess. "You can say it, don't worry. But we're used to it by now."

Sophie lets out a little breath.

"Well, Inner Haven will be quite the shock to you then," she says. "Now, I've been sent here today to get you clothed and briefed. So, shall we?"

"Sure, lead the way," I say.

Parked outside of the academy, we find a sleek, light grey transport, curved from head to toe and deliciously streamlined. It looks pristine, something that you can rarely say about the vehicles that litter the streets around here. After a day or two in the smog and mist, few vehicles remain clean.

This one, though, is obviously from Inner Haven, closed off from the elements. Inside, it's nicely furnished and comfortable, fitted with four white seats that face each other in the back. The front, meanwhile, consists of nothing but an electronic interface, with no facility for an actual person to drive.

"Take us to the southern quarter, Liberty Row," says Sophie.

Immediately, the vehicle comes to life, rumbling silently beneath us. Only rarely have I stepped foot in a transport of any kind. Mostly, I get around on foot or by use of the Conveyor Line.

Somehow, I don't particularly like the sensation of being driven by a computer. I sit uncomfortably for the first few minutes as the car sweeps onto the street, cruising in and out of traffic and avoiding pedestrians with great precision and skill. Computers are smart these days.

Tess, on the other hand, appears to enjoy the ride.

"Is this your car, Sophie?" she asks.

"Oh no, this is a government car, used for official business. We have one, but not as nice as this."

"We?"

"Oh, my husband and I. He's a Hawk."

"A Hawk? And…what are you?"

"Tess!" I say, cutting in. "Don't be rude."

"I'm not being rude," she says defensively. "I'm just asking a question."

Sophie laughs. "It's quite alright, really. Actually, I'm not an Enhanced at all. I'm an Unenhanced, just like you."

"What the…really?"

"Yes indeed. I was scouted by the Council of Matrimony and given an opportunity to '*marry up*', so to speak. That was three years ago now. I've lived in Inner Haven ever since."

Tess seems overly surprised by the news, but it's not completely alien to hear of such things. The Enhanced only have so many members, and frankly the risk of 'inbreeding' is far too high for them to only marry and procreate within their own ranks.

As such, they send scouts out to find suitable people – mostly women, given the higher number of male Enhanced – to marry their own members and diversify their bloodlines. Naturally, to be selected you have to be a fairly impressive person.

I suspect that Sophie's beauty had some part in it, but it's more likely that she's very smart too. Frankly, only intelligent people are considered suitable, while other qualities deemed important by the Court are also beneficial. A willingness to be compliant, and a fierce ambition to step up, and conform, to a higher class, are two such qualities.

Above all, however, is the ability to bear children who will themselves become members of the

Enhanced. Given how not all children carry the unique gifts of their parents, that one's something of a deal-breaker.

With that in mind, I ask Sophie whether she has any kids of her own.

"A baby boy, yes," she says proudly. "He's showing excellent signs that he'll be a Hawk, like his father."

Lucky for her. If he didn't, she'd most likely be relegated right back down to our ranks, whether her husband likes it or not.

As the journey continues, I begin to forget that the car is driving itself, and spend my time grilling Sophie on her life in Inner Haven. As far as I know it, members of the Enhanced can only marry members of the same type, or members of the Unenhanced deemed worthy. So, Hawks can marry Hawks, for example, but couldn't hook up with a Dasher or a Bat, who have amazing hearing.

This, apparently, is to prevent the illegal breeding of 'hybrids', genetic mutants who may carry several gifts and abilities.

"Oh yes, they hate any unsanctioned hybrid children," says Sophie. "Above all, it's the one thing that's not allowed."

"Why's that?" asks Tess.

"Well, it's not for me to say…" mumbles Sophie.

"And what do you mean by 'unsanctioned'," I ask. "So, as long as the breeding of hybrids is controlled, it's OK?"

"Let's change the subject, shall we, ladies?" says Sophie briskly. "We're venturing into the territory of rumours, and I don't like to gossip."

Funny that. She looks to be the exact sort of person who'd love to gossip.

Soon enough, the car is hurtling towards Liberty Row, and Sophie is preparing to step out. She probably hasn't had dealings with two curious girls like Tess and me for a long while, and given her position as an adopted member of the Enhanced, she knows she has to bite her tongue and not add to the rumours that spread through the city streets.

Personally, I don't think I could ever 'marry up' as she's done. They all seem like robots to me, people running on tracks like the Conveyor Line. All just doing their tasks, getting their jobs done, without asking questions or challenging the system.

From down here, that's all fine. We can whisper in quiet corners and moan and groan about the Court and the Consortium, and all the Savants who live and rule at the core of the city. But in Inner Haven, I doubt any such grumbling exists.

How boring it must be...

We step onto Liberty Row, not far south of Culture Corner, and Sophie leads us towards a shop called 'The Inner Circle'. Inside, the place is dressed up with fine garments and clothes: dresses and jackets and suits and hats and all manner of other items. What strikes me above all, however, is that they're all light blue, the same colour as the clothes Sophie is currently wearing.

"Not exactly a rainbow in here is it?" remarks Tess, looking unimpressed.

"Well it wouldn't be, would it," says Sophie. "Sky blue is the colour of all Unenhanced invited to live in Inner Haven."

"Ah…I get it. It's a way of determining social rank, right?" I ask.

"Well, yes, I suppose that's right," says Sophie. "This shop specialises in outfitting women, in particular, who are to 'marry up'. And if you're to visit Inner Haven, even for a day, you'll need to be wearing the right colour."

I see Tess rolling her eyes, and feel a giggle rise up through me. Sophie doesn't look impressed, but pushes on without drawing attention to it.

Instead, she sets about speaking with the shop assistant, who quickly comes rushing from the back.

"We need to set these two girls up in some fine dresses," says Sophie.

"Oh, congratulations," says the shop assistant, turning to us. "When are the big days?"

"Oh no, these two aren't getting married," laughs Sophie. "They're merely visiting Inner Haven for the day."

I don't enjoy the tone of her voice. It sounds like she's looking down on us. Or perhaps it's just my own insecurity. I can't really tell.

"OK, well one day perhaps you'll get lucky," says the assistant. "Come on girls, let's get started."

Lucky. It's not the word I'd use.

The next couple of hours are simply torturous. When you grow up dressed in hand-me-downs and rags, shopping in a fine outlet such as this is hardly second nature. In fact, shopping anywhere would make me a bit uncomfortable.

And yet both Tess and I are subjected to a dozen variations of outfits, stripped down and dressed up over and over again. The smile on Sophie's face suggests she's loving this, like we're her personal play dolls. This is probably a rare bit of fun for her, given the mundane life she must lead.

At the start, our opinions are asked for. After both Tess and I show an apparent lack and understanding of 'style', however, Sophie and the shop assistant begin making the decisions themselves.

Eventually, after much deliberation, they come to a decision, and the shop assistant sets about wrapping up two identical dresses for purchase.

"You do realise we have no money," says Tess.

"Of course. It's all taken care of, don't worry."

I choose not to look at the price tag to stop me from throwing up.

After we're done in the shop, Sophie leads us down the road to a beauty parlour. I know the women who parade around Culture Corner and the more expensive districts like to get all made up and looking pretty, but that's never been my world.

I guess I'm more comfortable in overalls and a pair of sturdy work boots.

Still, my early discomfort fades away as a team of beauty specialists begin working on my hair and face and nails, scrubbing and cutting and messaging me as I lie back in a chair and stare at the ceiling.

Sophie hovers about, pointing things out and giving the odd order. The women all acquiesce to anything she says, deferring to her higher standing if not her knowledge and expertise of beauty therapies. Any woman who has been known to marry up is certainly looked upon as special among our own class. Frankly, I just find her quite pretentious.

Once they're all done, the chair tilts back up and I look at myself in the mirror.

The change is astonishing, my hair just as beautiful as Sophie's now, my skin glowing, my hazed eyes popping. Everything has been trimmed and neatened up, the contours of my face clearer and more defined than ever before.

I look over at Tess, and see the same transformation. She's strikingly beautiful, enough to give Sophie a good run for her money. For a few moments, we stare at each other, as Sophie exclaims proudly: "You look positively stunning, ladies!"

I hate to admit it, but part of me agrees.

"Well girls, come on, what do you think?!"

If it wasn't for the many beauty therapists hovering around, longingly looking for approval, I'd probably just shrug and try to keep my reserve. However, I can't deny the job they've done, even if I do look completely alien to my own eyes.

"Brilliant," I say. "Thank you so much."

Tess offers up some similar compliment. More than me, she seems quite taken by her new look, her eyes fixed to her reflection and refusing to look away.

"Well, you'll fit in perfectly in Inner Haven looking like that," says Sophie. "Just try to make sure you don't mess up your hair too much tonight. I'll be able to touch it up tomorrow morning for you, but I can't work miracles." She turns to the therapists and distributes some money between them. "Thank you, ladies, for your fine work. I'll see you again soon."

As we leave the parlour, I ask her whether she comes down here a lot, given her comment to the women.

"Oh yes, my main role is to attend to women who are to marry a member of the Enhanced. Sometimes they need style and beauty tips, and to learn etiquette and such things."

"Why do they care about style and beauty over there?" I ask. "If you don't have emotion, what does it matter?"

"Well, that's an interesting point, Brie. It's true that the Savants are generally quite unemotional, but that's not necessarily true of the rest of the Enhanced. And, the Savants still consider beauty to be beneficial if it means making the Enhanced happy."

"Sounds a bit superficial to me."

"It is, but there's nothing wrong with that. You should embrace your beauty, Brie, and not question it. There's nothing wrong with looking good if it makes you feel good too."

I can't tell, at this point, if I'm just choosing to question her for the sake of it. There's just something about her that grates on me, this air of superiority that she probably doesn't even realise she carries around with her.

Then again, can I blame her for that? If you're specifically chosen to marry into the ranks of the Enhanced, you're going to feel pretty special, right?

The remainder of the afternoon involves a briefing about etiquette and the format of the following day's events. We take up position in a little café, nestled in the corner of a quiet courtyard in one of the more prosperous parts of Outer Haven.

There, Sophie gives us an extensive run down of our expected behaviours, things that anyone with common sense should naturally do anyway. Yet, given how we're 'nothing but Unenhanced', the Court have seen fit to clarify the most basic of conducts and manners.

Personally, I find it insulting.

"Yes, I know it's all rather basic stuff," remarks Sophie, "but it's my role to take you through it regardless."

I yawn, sit back, and zone out until she has something more interesting to say.

That comes when she tells us how the ceremony

will go.

"It will take place at the base of the High Tower, upon a large open square. Now, there will be screens, and it will be televised, so be prepared to be famous."

Oh God…

"Why are they televising it?" I ask.

"Because it's a ceremony to honour the Unenhanced," says Sophie. "So, it stands to reason that the population of Outer Haven get to witness it."

"Well maybe they should have just had the ceremony *in* Outer Haven," I suggest.

A stupid suggestion. Like the members of the Court want to come down here…

"That would defeat the purpose of it all. The honour itself is in visiting Inner Haven. This way, all the people get to see it."

"Great. The kids at the academy are going to have a field day with this," I say to Tess, who laughs in response.

And on Sophie goes, telling us about the rest of the day. The timings of the ceremony, the little tour we'll get around the grounds of Inner Haven, the feast that will follow and the people who are likely to show up.

Unfortunately, my mind is now busy with the thought of being shown across the entire city. At heart, I'm hardly the showiest of girls. And now,

I'm going to be on display to the world.

Sophie needn't worry about me messing up my hair tonight.

I doubt I'll sleep a wink.

CHAPTER NINE

The morning of the ceremony follows a night of nerves.

I'm exhausted.

When I look in the cracked and partially stained mirror in my room, I don't see the beautiful girl from yesterday looking back. My eyes are heavy and dark. My skin has lost its glow. Only my hair remains intact, although even that needs some tidying up.

My mentality has changed too. Suddenly, knowing that I'm going to be seen by the entire city has made me consider my appearance more closely. Given how I'm at the age where I might start looking for a suitable husband, this could be an opportunity to make a good impression.

More importantly, it's an opportunity to *not* make a bad one. Knowing my luck, that's the more likely scenario.

When Tess wakes, she appears to be suffering from no such problems. Her hair, shorter than mine, looks like it needs no more than a quick comb and a bit of spray. Her eyes are bright and blue – they'll surely look great with her dress – and her skin remains nicely clear and lacking in any redness or blemishes.

It's obvious that nerves aren't a problem for her. That's more my domain. She's not the most social of girls, but she's certainly got a deep well of inner confidence flowing through her. Rarely do you see her get flustered. Today will likely put that to the test.

Sophie arrives early, as she said she would, in order to get us prepared for the ceremony before escorting us over to Inner Haven. She's ushered into the academy by Mrs Carmichael, who leads her up to the second floor where we dwell.

I find them out in the corridor, two women at either end of both the social and aesthetic spectrum: Sophie, all bright and beautiful, living her perfectly manicured life in Inner Haven; Mrs Carmichael, old and bitter, never more happy than when she's sucking on a cigarette and drowning her head in whiskey.

I do remember a time when she herself was quite easy on the eye. As a little girl, I considered her quite attractive, relatively speaking of course, especially given her advanced years. The death of Mr Carmichael, however, precipitated an already quickening decline into the haggard old lady who stands before me today, yellow of teeth and sallow of skin.

I wouldn't have her any other way.

As I enter into the corridor, the two diametrically opposed women appear to be involved in a fairly frosty exchange. Mostly, the frost comes from my guardian, Sophie's more buoyant nature insufficient to keep the cold at bay.

It's no surprise, given Mrs Carmichael's feelings towards the residents of Inner Haven. She has no tolerance for any woman who thinks themselves above their station.

"Ah, Brie," says Sophie as she sees me, seemingly happy for the interruption. "Did you sleep OK?"

"Does it look like I slept OK?" I ask sarcastically.

"Hmmm, yes there's some work that needs doing. Mrs Carmichael, if you'd excuse me. Thank you for allowing me into your home."

"I didn't exactly have any say in the matter," mumbles Mrs Carmichael, turning back towards her own room.

Sophie ignores the jibe and breezily comes forward. I step back and allow her into my room. Tess sits up in bed, rubbing her eyes and yawning.

"Hey, Soph," she says after the long intake of air. "How's my hair looking?"

"Rather good, actually," says Sophie, looking quite surprised. She looks to me again. "You need a little more work, Brie. Let's get started, shall we."

Sophie moves towards my bed and lays down a briefcase. Opening it up, I see that she's brought along a mobile beauty parlour of some kind, filled with all sorts of combs and brushes and other utensils, as well as make up and hair spray and various products used to turn an ugly ducking into a swan.

I always find it amazing how people can alter their appearance so drastically with a bit of powder and paint. And not just the women. The more artistically inclined men down at Culture Corner will commonly dress themselves up too.

Setting to work, Sophie rambles on again about the etiquette of the day as she puts me back in order.

Mostly, we're told to walk upright and straight, and to hold our hands neatly to our sides. Posture, it seems, is considered important in identifying higher class citizens. Anyone caught slouching or crossing their arms whilst in public are immediately reprimanded by *'posture police'*.

Yes, they actually have those.

Our expressions, too, need to be reigned in. Tess and I know as much from speaking with Deputy Burns that the Savants aren't exactly expressive with their facial movements. The rest of the Enhanced, by the sounds of things, are required to adhere to that doctrine.

"Smiling is allowed, of course," says Sophie. "It's considered a friendly expression, and so beneficial."

"Not so friendly when Deputy Burns tries it," jokes Tess. "He looks seriously creepy."

Sophie laughs awkwardly.

"Some Savants have trouble with it, although many of them look natural," she says. "Especially the lower ranked ones. They're usually less detached and have a little more emotion."

"So the higher up you go, the more cold and weird

they are?" I ask. "I can't imagine what the members of the Consortium must look like trying to crack a smile."

Tess laughs loudly. Sophie looks like she's about to frown, but holds the expression back.

"So, what expressions are *disallowed*?" I ask, struggling to ask the question in a serious manner.

"I did go through this yesterday, Brie. Don't you remember?"

"I zoned out," I admit.

She sucks in an exasperated breath.

"Well, OK then. Simply put, anything negative is undesirable. So frowning, gritting your teeth, shaking your head, things like that. Just smile and nod and everything will be fine."

"Must be exhausting," remarks Tess.

Sophie doesn't counter the claim.

Soon enough, our makeovers are complete. As expected, mine took a fair bit longer than Tess's. We step to the mirror and admire Sophie's work, my face once more bright and glowing and my hair suitably glossy.

"OK, into the dresses please, ladies," says Sophie.

We slip into the sky blue dresses bought for us the day before. I wonder if we're going to get to keep them after, but don't ask. Frankly, I can't think of a single occasion where I'd put this thing back on.

Once dressed, Sophie brings forward some

matching shoes. They look quite basic, flat on the sole and without any embellishments. I slide on my pair. They're much too big.

"Not to worry," says Sophie, leaning down.

She presses against the side of the shoe down by the big toe. Slowly, it begins to shrink in size until it fits perfectly.

"Better?" she asks.

"Um...yeah," I say.

I wasn't aware that such shoes existed. If only my work boots had the same function.

It doesn't end there, though. At the rear of the shoe, she presses again, and a heel extends from the bottom of the sole. Up I go, gaining an inch in height, then two, then three. Soon, I'm struggling to keep my footing.

"You have worn heels before, yes?" asks Sophie.

We both shake our heads.

She leans back in and takes the heel down a bit.

"How about that? Try them out."

We both do a little walk around the room, then out into the corridor. A couple of the other residents of the top floor giggle as they watch our little catwalk display. I feel completely foolish, even here. I can't imagine how I'm going to feel being watched by the entire city.

After a few goes up and down, however, I manage to walk without tripping over. Still, I feel like I must look like a deer on ice.

Or Mrs Carmichael after one too many whiskeys…

"You'll get the hang of it," says Sophie.

Clearly she has more confidence in my abilities than I do. Tess, meanwhile, appears suspiciously adept from the word go.

"You sure you haven't worn these before?" I ask.

She shrugs and smiles cheekily. "It's all about balance, Brie. You'll get it…eventually. Hopefully by this afternoon."

Her little wink is unwelcome.

Damn you and your natural balance.

Unfortunately, I have little extra time to practice.

"Come now, girls, we need to get going. We're already a good few minutes past schedule."

She sounds worried. Clearly keeping us right on track is her priority today, and if she doesn't see through that function, there might be hell to pay.

Before we go, however, Mrs Carmichael emerges from her den and looks upon us both with a smile.

"You look lovely, girls, you truly do. You'll make fine wives to two very lucky men some day."

"I completely agree, Mrs Carmichael," says Sophie. "Looking like that, they'll be sure to impress the residents of Inner Haven."

I'm not sure that was what our guardian was

getting at. She doesn't correct Sophie, though, and merely tells us good luck. Then, as Tess and Sophie begin making their way down the corridor, she steps in towards me.

"Have you taken your medication today, Brie?" she asks quietly.

"Oh..no!" I say. "I've been so busy this morning I forgot."

"Well, do it now, quick," she says.

I dash into my room, open my bedside table, and pop a couple of pills. My stocks appear to be running low, something Mrs Carmichael notes.

"I'll pick up some more for you at the black market," she says.

I don't much like her going there. The black market exists in the northern quarter, a necessary location in order to keep it under the radar.

I'm pulled into a very brief hug, as Sophie calls "what's the hold up?" from down the corridor.

Neither of us answer.

Instead, Mrs Carmichael's eyes narrow. "Be careful today," she whispers. "Don't trust anyone over there, do you understand?"

I nod.

"Of course, Mrs Carmichael. Don't worry…I'll be back later."

I leave her there, and wander down the corridor towards the other two. Her paranoia and distrust of

Inner Haven, and the Savants in particular, isn't something new.

Still, they serve to make me even more nervous than I was before. Hardly the best pep talk, really.

Downstairs, the residents of the academy have gathered to see us off. The girls swarm around us and tell us how pretty we look, as Sophie tries to stop too many of them from tugging at our dresses, slapping away grubby hands and ushering us quickly on.

The little boys stand back, giggling, while the older ones look on at us admiringly. When I catch them staring, they blush and turn away.

I lock eyes with Drum for a moment, who stands at the back with a sheepish look on his face. He flashes that smile that only I ever see, and mouths 'good luck', before returning his eyes to his feet.

Before we even get to the door, I can feel the draft of cold morning air whistling through. When the door opens, and we step outside, it becomes evidently clear that these dresses are going to be woefully insufficient in keeping us warm.

"Don't worry, you'll be fine in Inner Haven," says Sophie, watching us shiver as we step into the car. It appears to be the same one as yesterday.

This time, I'm not so daunted when Sophie gives the order, and the vehicle begins moving off of its own accord.

"Western gate to Inner Haven," she says.

I feel a thrill at the words.

From the centre of the western quarter, we begin moving eastwards towards the middle of the city. I've travelled these streets a thousand times before, and know them like the back of my hand. When I was young, I'd creep as close to the wall as I could manage, get right up to its base and imagine what the world was like on the other side.

Today, I'll find out.

The wall isn't overly tall, a couple of storey high perhaps. It's thick, though, and built from iron, a perfect circle surrounding Inner Haven with four entry points at the north, south, east and west. At each entry point, large gates provide passage to the two parts of the city, manned by members of the City Guard.

We move beyond the colourful, vibrant streets of Outer Haven, drenched in neon and filled with life, and up a straight road that leads to the wall. Immediately, the transition becomes apparent, the street turning quiet and drab as it stretches towards the core of the city.

When we reach the wall, a door to the side of the gate opens, and a Brute steps through, dressed in his armour and with the badge of the city at the top of his chest. He's enormous, ducking his head slightly to move through the door, which clearly wasn't built with such colossal men in mind.

Sophie gives the order for the right hand window to open, and it swiftly retracts into the door of the vehicle.

"Name and identification number," says the Brute,

his voice booming from his mountainous chest.

"Sophie Winchester. I.D. HKW-193. I'm here to escort two Unenhanced to the ceremony this afternoon. They're to be honoured for their role in the terrorist attack."

The Brute raises a monstrous arm and taps Sophie's information into an interface on his inner forearm.

Then he nods.

"Proceed," he says.

He steps back, and the gate ahead begins to open, splitting from the middle and winding into the metal wall. I try to peer ahead to get a good look, but the front window is narrow.

Sophie takes note and rectifies the situation.

"Activate transparency mode," she says.

The vehicle's computer takes action. Immediately, the external shell of the car seems to fade, the sleek grey seeming to melt into the air. I reach up and touch the ceiling to make sure it's still there, and feel that the surface remains solid.

"Hopefully that'll give you a better view," says Sophie, smiling. "In Inner Haven, there's no need for us to hide."

I stare forward, the top half of the car now almost completely see-through, and get my first proper look at Inner Haven. As the car begins moving through the gate, my eyes are immediately drawn to the towers ahead, all of them the same height, same shape, same colour. It's as if they were clones of each other, lined up along the street, clean and pristine and glimmering under the morning sun.

"Activate tour," says Sophie. "Follow the Spiral."

The car moves forward away from the gate, turning onto a wide and open street that curves around the boundary of Inner Haven alongside the wall. As we go, Sophie turns into a tour guide - a part she probably plays a lot with her clients – telling us about the structure of Inner Haven and its component parts.

It seems it works in a spiral, something I wasn't aware of. Here, the main street flows around the boundary of the city, curving gently in until it arrives at the High Tower right at the city's core. It's a simple structure, that allows for only one major street, with smaller ones spreading out in all directions from the core to provide quicker passage to the various districts.

The spiral works, unsurprisingly, to help determine class. On the outside coils, the members of the Enhanced who marry Unenhanced live. Further in, you'll find single members of the Enhanced, followed by Enhanced who have married partners of their same kind.

The innermost coils, closest to the High Tower, are reserved for the more lowly Savants and members of the Court. The High Tower itself, however, is home to higher class Savants and Courtiers, with the summit occupied by the Consortium.

Many floors of the High Tower, as well as many buildings across Inner Haven, are used for working purposes too. Here, the main trades are science and engineering, where the supreme intellects of the Savants are put to good use, ably supported by the Enhanced and their useful physical improvements.

We drive around the main street, slowly but surely circling in. I look out at the streets and note that they're fairly quiet and still. There's no trash, no art, no colour. All the buildings are drenched in sleek tones of grey and white, so different from the vibrant melting plot on the other side of the wall.

No advertising displays fill the sides of buildings, no neon lights spill down and saturate the air with their multi-coloured glow. What colour there is belongs to the Unenhanced who have come here, women like Sophie who drift about, upright and tall, in their sky blue dresses and suits.

It's like an alien world, one devoid of life. A place of order where everyone seems to wander to the beat of an imaginary drum, all walking at the same pace as they pass to work and back. Calm and serene, I feel like I've entered a weird dream just looking at the place.

The look on Tess's face suggests she's thinking exactly the same as me. Truthfully, I don't see how anyone who's come from Outer Haven couldn't.

"It's strange, isn't it," remarks Sophie. "Strange to your eyes."

We both nod together.

"Everyone who sees it for the first time thinks the same. But there's a charm to the quiet here, a sense of calm that I could no longer live without. Everyone comes round eventually."

Looking at the streets, I don't see how that's possible. *I'd have to get a lobotomy to be able to stomach it here.*

We continue to circle, drawing closer to the core, the High Tower appearing between gaps in buildings and teasing us as it continually flashes and disappears. The buildings, too, most of them apartments, grow more grand, larger allowances of space provided to the higher ranked members of the city.

"What's the point of having all that space?" I ask Sophie. "The Savants don't care for art. They'll just have bigger blank walls to stare at."

Sophie gives a hint that she agrees. I see it in the twitch in her eye. Naturally, she has a pre-programmed response, though.

"It's a status symbol, Brie. It shows importance, influence."

Still, I wonder if that even matters to them. Where is the line drawn? So, they don't feel emotions, and therefore can't love, or hate, or feel fear or joy. So why does status matter? Status, surely, gives a feeling of pride, perhaps of superiority. Do they feel those things?

I don't bother Sophie with the query, since she'll just give me a canned response. Most likely, they're

110

not entirely devoid of emotion, just severely lacking in it.

I mean, surely if a Savant had to watch their parents die, as Tess did, they'd feel some grief at the loss, some anger at the perpetrators, some desire for revenge?

And if they don't, then surely they can't be human. Some higher evolution in their own minds, perhaps. Higher in some ways, lower in others.

For me, it's culture that sets us aside from the rest of the birds and the beasts. If it's just survival and proliferating the species that matters to them, then they have more in common with cockroaches than they do with us over in Outer Haven.

As my mind rumbles on, the car does so too, albeit as silently as the streets around us. Soon, Sophie is drawing our attention to the front as the car curves around the final bend.

Ahead, the High Tower comes into full view for the first time, stretching up to the heavens. It looks so much more imposing up close, its base wide and circular, its domed roof disappearing into the low hanging clouds.

The street finally goes straight as it leads towards its foundations, set up with towering stands with tiered seating on either side. Between them, a stage awaits, sitting within an open square before the many glass doors that lead into the building. And all over, huge screens have been erected, ready to broadcast the ceremony across the city.

Above the stage, several storeys high, a balcony extends out from the High Tower, looking down upon the world below. White chairs adorn it, waiting to be occupied by only a dozen men and women.

And in the middle, one stands out more distinguished than the rest.

"Who sits there?" asks Tess, staring at the balcony, her eyes dazzled by the scene ahead.

"Oh, didn't I tell you?" says Sophie. "The Consortium will be in attendance, watching from up there."

My heart thuds. I had no idea they cared…

"And the middle chair…" continues Sophie, bristling with excitement. "Well, that will be occupied by Director Cromwell, the Consortium's senior member. I hope you girls know what an honour that is."

I look upon the scene again, and the word 'honour' doesn't register.

Fear. Nerves. Deep anxieties.

Those are all far more appropriate.

CHAPTER TEN

"I didn't even realise the Consortium had a senior member," Tess is saying as the car curves into an underground parking garage to the side of the road. "So, this Director Cromwell is their boss?"

"I suppose you could say that," says Sophie. "He's their elected leader. The members of the Consortium are all the most prominent people in the city, leaders of its various committees and operations. His job is to oversee them all."

We pull to a stop against a wall, sliding up against other similar looking vehicles. As we do, the walls of the car once more take shape, losing their transparency.

"So, what now?" asks Tess.

"Now, we wait. The ceremony will be beginning soon enough. But before then, let's take a stroll. Give you a closer look around."

"Sounds good to me."

I follow the two of them out as they continue to converse, Tess seeming oddly undaunted by what we've just seen. Frankly, I can't even begin to imagine what it's going to be like out there when the stands are full, and all eyes are on me.

I shudder and send the thought to the rear of my mind as I jog to catch the others up.

When we emerge outside of the parking garage and onto the city streets, it quickly dawns on me how warm it is. Outside of the academy, it was freezing wearing only this dress. Here, it feels like a regular spring day.

"Underfloor heating," Sophie says, tapping her heeled foot on the ground. "It's the same across Inner Haven. The temperate is based on scientific evidence for the ideal heat for happiness and productivity."

"I'm starting to see the appeal of living here," jokes Tess, a vocal hater of the cold.

Oddly, though, the warmer air feels out of sync with the surroundings. The entire aesthetic here is cold and lifeless, a place that fits in perfectly with the detached demeanour of the Savants. It's clear that this place was designed by, and for, such people.

I actually feel sorry for the rest of the Enhanced who have to endure it. At least in Outer Haven, for all its problems and dangers, there's some vivacity and soul to the streets and districts, a lived-in feel that serves to animate the world. Here, it's dull and empty and there's a cold that no amount of underfloor heating can fix.

We wander a little closer to the High Tower, and from various avenues and side streets I see people beginning to gather. All wear similar clothing: men in suits similar to that worn by Deputy Burns,

114

women in dresses with cardigans and jackets. The colours range from dark tones of grey to light, with plenty of sky blue on show as well.

I immediately feel some affinity with those wearing the latter, knowing they were once, like me, living across the wall. Those with the darker tones of grey I can get on board with too – they'll be regular Enhanced, modified and evolved, but still human.

Those in light grey, however, are the aliens to me. Savants with their detached eyes and cold stares. How I'd like to get inside one of their heads and have a fiddle about, see what the hell they're thinking.

As the people gather, and begin hovering into position, it becomes evidently clear that the concept of hierarchy and class are once more at play.

Like with the living arrangements here, the Unenhanced are afforded the worst viewing positions at the rear of the stands, furthest from the stage. Then, the order is once more based upon an Enhanced's particular worth, with Savants of the Court given the best positioning, and their most esteemed members right at the front.

The show of colour, or lack thereof, is actually quite fascinating. From the sky blue at the back, to the darker tones of grey, all the way to the lightest of greys at the front. It's one of the only things I've seen here that's actually quite striking and beautiful.

It does draw a question to my lips, though.

"Can Unenhanced marry Savants?" I ask. "Or do they only marry among themselves?"

Somehow, their natural air of superiority makes me think it's the latter.

"No, Unenhanced can marry them," Sophie informs me. "However, it's usually quite rare, and only the most exceptional of Unenhanced are given such an honour."

Honour? Being married to a cold, heartless Savant is hardly what I'd consider an honour. Jeez, they've really done a number of Sophie over here, haven't they...

"Naturally," continues Sophie, "given the limited numbers of Savants, breeding with Unenhanced is something that's unavoidable. However, mostly they try to manage with what they have."

"Can't they just, I don't know, make more Savants?" asks Tess. "You know, like they did hundreds of years ago, when they were first created. Why do they bother breeding them naturally?"

"Because, as far as I know, the natural resources aren't available for such things," answers Sophie. "I'm sure if they could simply create modified people they would. It would certainly be a lot easier."

"Well, lucky for us they can't," I say. "If they could do that, I'm sure we'd eventually become extinct..."

For a brief second, Sophie's eyebrows drop into a questioning frown. Then, remembering herself, they rise up again and that inane smile returns.

"Enough of that talk, Brie. Let's change the subject, and please, make sure you smile and don't frown so much. Remember what we talked about."

I plant the biggest smile I can on my face and look straight at her. She rolls her eyes and shakes her head.

"Ah, caught you!" I say. "No negative expressions, Sophie...remember!"

Tess laughs loudly. Sophie struggles to prevent her expression from turning even more sour. And for the first time, my smile becomes genuine.

As the square begins to fill more quickly, Sophie leads us over towards the right where I notice a few other men and women, all dressed in sky blue, have gathered. Our guide appears to know several of them, quickening her step – in a suitable manner, and maintaining perfect posture, of course – to meet them.

As we mesh into a group, it becomes clear that these are the other Unenhanced here to be honoured, along with their guides. By the looks on the people's faces, it's obvious which are which.

The guides are all very much like Sophie, smiling constantly and holding their posture perfectly. The rest are more like Tess and me, staring around in awe and looking quite out of place.

As we stand there, the various guides perform some quick introductions. I shake hands and try to see if I recognise anyone. One man stands out from the video footage. If I recall correctly, he went charging straight into the fray at about the same time as Tess and me.

Brave souls, all of them.

Truth be told, the honour today is not in being invited here to Inner Haven. Nor is it in meeting any of the luminaries I'm sure to encounter later. Certainly, I have no feelings whatsoever about being looked down on, literally, by the Consortium and Director Cromwell.

No. For me, the true honour in today is meeting these brave people. It's a trait that the Savants seem to admire, but can never possess.

Because to be brave, you need to first feel fear.

As we stand in our huddle, watching the huge square fill with a sea of people, a familiar face appears.

"Good to see you all here today," says Deputy Burns, wandering towards us from near the front stage.

Immediately, the guides stand up even more firmly and turn completely still. One or two of the Outer Haveners attempt to do the same. The rest of us just stand there like normal human beings.

"As you will have been told, I will be presenting the ceremony today, seeing as I've met you all already. You will be called up, one by one, and presented with a ceremonial plaque. I may also invite you to answer a question or two…"

Jesus Christ. Did I zone out during that bit too?

118

"Now, I can sense a lot of nerves among you. There is no need for them. This is your day, and you should enjoy it. Your seats are reserved for you over to the right of the stage, set out in alphabetical order."

I glance at Tess. With a surname like Bradbury, she might well be up first.

Better to get it out of the way early, rather than endure the wait.

"Well, good luck to you all. And remember, the world is watching."

Great. What a way to sign off to a bunch of nervous people. I thought these Savants were meant to be super-smart?

Deputy Burns moves off, now without his guard of Brutes - here, there's no such need for them – and moves towards the side of the stage. With a little prodding from our guides, we follow, moving right to the front and a little section of seating set out beneath the stands.

"OK girls, this is where I leave you," says Sophie. "I'll be seeing you after. Good luck!"

Off she goes, along with the others, leaving behind a rather confused trail of ten or so Outer Haveners. We move towards the seats, and see that our names are laid out on them. I glance to the front to see that Tess is, as it turns out, up first.

"Nervous?" she asks me.

"I'm fine," I lie. "Don't set the bar too high up there."

She laughs as she wanders over to take her seat, and I drop into mine about two thirds of the way down the line.

From the shadows beneath the stage, we're pretty much out of sight of the crowd above. I'm happy for that. I had a vague idea that we might all be seated up on the stage, all lined up for so many thousands of eyes to inspect.

Instead, I just need to get my time on stage out of the way. Then I can relax. A bit of socialising here, some chit-chat there, and I'll be back home before I know it.

From our position, however, the stage is visible, straight off to the left. We all watch as Deputy Burns appears, walking towards a little podium in the same efficient yet rigid fashion that everyone here seems to adopt.

He attempts another of his odd smiles as he goes, his lips rising but his eyes remaining flat. When he reaches the podium, he stands straight and turns his head to the left, then right, like some sort of robot.

Behind him, a giant screen shows a close up of his face, giving those at the back a better view of his awkward attempts to display emotion. I just hope the more easily frightened kids aren't watching this back at the academy. It's the sort of thing that will give them nightmares.

"Good afternoon to you all," he begins, his voice booming through a microphone hovering above the podium. "To all of you present here, and to all of you watching across Outer Haven, I offer you a warm welcome. Today, we are here to celebrate ten brave men and women who acted valiantly in the face of adversity, and to further extend the hand of friendship across the two parts of this great city."

He pauses suddenly for dramatic effect. It's jarring. And yet the crowd begin to applaud, clapping in unison, prompted to do so by signs that light up with instructions on either side of the stage.

When the signs turn from 'Applaud' to 'Stop', the clapping ends abruptly. It's unnatural and odd, but very much in keeping with what I've seen around here.

Deputy Burns continues as soon as a complete silence has fallen once more.

"Before we meet our special guests, let me introduce you to our most esteemed members of the Court. Please welcome, the Consortium."

More canned applause begins as I look up and see several men and women appear at the balcony above, several storeys up from the stage. They line up, all dressed in pure white, looking down upon the crowd with empty eyes. They appear to have little interest in attempting a false smile.

It's such a rare sight to see them, these people behind the curtain who pull all the strings. It speaks volumes of this event that they're here, displaying themselves to the public in a show of solidarity. It suggests that they're taking the threat of the Fanatics seriously.

In their centre, I see the man who must be Director

Cromwell, his hair neat and short and almost as white as his suit. Like all men I've seen here, he has no facial hair, his skin pale and yet strikingly smooth given his age.

In fact, were it not for his elderly hands, wrinkled as they are, I'd consider him a much younger man. The same goes for many of the Savants, their faces so lacking in expression that wrinkles are less inclined to develop.

There's little to differentiate him from the other members of the Consortium but for the small letter 'D' that sits within the centre of his insignia. Like all city officials and servants, he wears the badge of Haven below his collar, the inner circle coloured white to indicate that he's a Savant. On his badge, however, there's a little 'D' in the middle, while the rest of the Consortium have the letter 'C'.

For a brief moment, the cameras show them all, standing up on their balcony, displayed to the whole of the city across the giant screens that dot it. I look closely at the huge screen behind Deputy Burns as a fresh applause greets their entry, inspecting them closely before the cameras once more centre on our presenter for the day.

The applause dies again, and Deputy Burns continues.

"Three days ago, a terrible atrocity was committed in Outer Haven, at its centre of art and music. We here in Inner Haven are all horrified by this event, and are here today to not only celebrate those who acted so bravely, but to assure you all that everything is being done to prevent any further loss of life.

"This city stands alone as a beacon of hope for all people. Here, we are dedicated to the sole aim of rebuilding this world that has seen so much chaos and turmoil. The fate of the people living here is paramount to us. We will not tolerate wanton acts of destruction and murder."

He stops, and turns his head to the left, his eyes levelling on us all hidden away in the shadows.

"Now, without further ado, let me introduce our first special guest. Please welcome, Tess Bradbury, a labourer from the western quarter."

I feel my heart thud as Tess stands up. The world goes deathly silent for a second. Then, when Tess steps into the light, the signs come to life with the word 'Applaud', and the artificial clapping fills the air again.

I can barely watch as Tess wanders up to the stage, moving with grace given the unfamiliar heels she's wearing. She looks calm and assured, her face glowing bright with a smile on the big screen as the cameras follow her towards the podium.

When she arrives at Deputy Burn's side, he reaches out with his hand and she takes it. Then, from the other side of the stage, a young woman appears carrying a small commemorative plaque. It's passed to Deputy Burns, who hands it straight over to Tess.

"Congratulations, Tess. It's quite fitting that you

are first up, seeing as you were one of the first on the scene to help. Tell us all, how did you *feel* when you saw the devastation?"

The little microphone hovers over from Deputy Burns's mouth to Tess's. She seems to think for a moment, but somehow maintains her smile, fading a little but still clinging to her face.

Then she speaks, breaking the short silence.

"I felt…like I needed to help," she says, her voice spreading and echoing down the wide street. "There was blood everywhere. People were screaming. I wanted to help wherever I could."

Deputy Burns nods.

"And you did. Bravo. A fantastic job."

This time, the crowd appear to begin applauding before the signs have lit. Tess smiles again, brighter this time, and the camera zooms closer onto her gorgeous face.

"And can I just say," she calls over the din, "that it's such an honour to be invited here to your wonderful city."

The applause grows louder. Deputy Burns's smile threatens to become genuine. And with a little bow, Tess cups her plaque to her chest and is ushered from the stage, soaking up the adoration, false or otherwise, of the masses as she goes.

I shake my head, happy that Sophie isn't there to reprimand me.

Damn it Tess, I told you not to set the bar too

high...

CHAPTER ELEVEN

Before it gets to me, four further Outer Haveners are called up to the stage.

I barely focus on their introductions, and the very brief interviews that Deputy Burns conducts. I'm too nervous right now to do anything but focus on myself.

By the time the middle-aged man next to me steps up into the limelight, my chest has gone as tight as a drum, and my heart is pulsing with such ferocity that I fear it might well break free from its confines.

My eyes shift in all directions, and my breathing rattles along at a frightening speed. Through my muddled hearing, I'm just about aware of the voices on the stage, and the applause of the crowd.

I focus as hard as I can, take several deep breaths to control my rapid intake of air, and blink hard several times in an attempt to reacquire my vision. Then, as the latest applause fades, I look to see Deputy Burns turning to look at me.

"So, who's next," he says. "Ah, yes, we met the charming Tess Bradbury a few minutes ago. Now, it's her partner in crime, Brie Melrose."

A new applause begins, and I stand shakily to my

feet. Suddenly, my heels feel like they're about ten inches high, my body trembling as I take my first steps towards the light.

Come on, Brie, get it together.

Just act like Tess did. You don't want to look a fool, do you?

My little internal pep talk has some effect. I stop for the briefest of seconds in the shadows, take a final breath, straighten up my posture and plant a smile on my face.

Somehow, it seems to do the trick.

Then, I step into the light, and around the corner the wide street and high stands come into view. A sea of faces greet me, all melting into one and spreading far into the distance.

Above the stands, large screens televise my every move, some providing wider angles as I walk, others zooming closer to my face. I note the nerves in my eyes and attempt to lighten up my smile, before turning my attention straight on Deputy Burns ahead.

I manage to reach him without tripping or falling over. I consider that a small victory.

I'm greeted by his unnatural grin, although I've seen it enough by now to not be put off by it. At least he's trying, which is more than can be said for the Consortium above, casting their dull eyes down on me as they trace my steps.

I take Deputy Burns's hand as I arrive at the podium, and the applause begins to quieten as my plaque is brought out and presented. I take it, happy to have something for my hands to do, and see that it's nothing but a basic sheet of metal with an engraving of my name on the front, along with the date and location of the attack, and the number of people I helped.

Apparently, it was 8. I hadn't realised.

When the applause dies, an eerie silence follows. I turn again to look at the crowd, and notice how still everything is, how quiet. Even from towards the back, the tiniest shuffle can be seen and heard.

My eyes shift up again, and I see my giant face plastered across the screens. My smile appears to have evaporated. I quickly revive it, but it doesn't look as natural and relaxed as Tess's did.

Deputy Burns's voice breaks the strange calm.

"Well, Brie, congratulations. How does it feel to be here in Inner Haven? Are you as enthused about the place as your friend?"

I nod, and try to speak, but my words fail me. A second attempt brings a nervous croak from my throat.

"I am," I say. "It's an honour to be here."

"The honour is ours," says Deputy Burns magnanimously. "Now tell us, Brie, what life is like in Outer Haven?"

I take a breath, and try to hold my trembling body together. My mind rushes fast. I don't know what do say.

In the end, I give these people what I think they want.

"It's loud and busy," I say. "Not calm and tranquil like it is here."

"I can attest to that," adds Deputy Burns. "The two parts of this city are very different, and have their own unique charms."

Damn, why couldn't I have put it like that...

"It sounds like you'd like to live here one day," he adds. "Do you think you'd fit in?"

I'm in a corner here.

"I hope so," I say. "But that's not for me to decide."

"Quite right. However, I'm sure there are many young bachelors here who would love to wed a brave and beautiful girl like you."

Another silence. I see my stupid, awkward smile on the big screen. The camera seems to be drawing in closer, picking up every little detail, every tick and movement of my eyes.

"It would be an honour," I manage to say.

"That it would. Thank you again, Brie, for your courage and cool head. I hope you enjoy the remainder of your time here."

He extends his hand again, and I unpeel one set of fingers from my plaque.

As I take a grip of his rigid digits, however, a strange sound of static begins to crackle.

129

My eyes drift to the nearest screen to see that the image of my face has lost its focus. I turn to the other screens to see that they're similarly afflicted, the images fading and turning an odd, distorted mix of grey and white and black.

A murmur begins to spread through the crowd as all eyes pick out one screen or another.

"What's going on?" asks Deputy Burns away from the mic, looking to a technician just off the stage.

The man shrugs, before tapping away at an interface in an attempt to decipher the problem.

"Apologies for the delay, ladies and gentlemen," announces the Deputy. "We appear to be having some technical troubles. We'll have them sorted momentarily."

The crowd continue to murmur, whispering now among themselves. I stand there, still rooted to the spot, wondering if I should move away or not.

Suddenly, the hissing and buzzing grows louder, biting and scratching at my ears. I grimace at the sound and shut my eyes.

It ends abruptly.

The square goes silent once more but for the collective hum of the audience. My eyes open and turn again to the screens. A ripple of confusion swells.

What's going on?

On the screens now, all is dark. But in the centre, a silhouette remains, blacker than the background, and in the shape of a man.

I turn to Deputy Burns, who looks at the image with the bare whisker of a reaction. But there's something there: a little frown, a sharper glint in his usually detached eyes.

Then, rumbling out from the screens, a strange, modulated voice echoes.

"I speak on behalf of the *Nameless*," it says loudly. "And I speak directly to the oppressed, to all those living across Outer Haven."

From the corner of my eye, I see Deputy Burns march off to the side of the stage. He talks sharply to the technician, barking orders.

"Your lives are a lie," continues the voice. "Your freedom is false. Do not give in to fear. The Fanatics are not who you think they are…"

More static burns in my ears. The Deputy hovers over the technician, who taps furiously on the interface.

Through the static, the voice continues, more difficult to hear now as the technician works to sever the connection.

"We are your friends. We are your salvation. The day of reckoning is coming…"

Across the stage, I hear the technician announce: "Got it."

As he does, the screens all fade to black once more, cutting off the mysterious voice. Then, flickering, they light up bright. And fill again with my face.

I'm still staring at the screen as my face reappears. I'm certainly not smiling anymore. I'm just staring, and looking pretty dumb, with a heavy frown cutting off half my eyes.

It takes me a moment to properly see myself. I turn to look at Deputy Burns, who comes hurrying back over to me. His weird smile is even more forced than usual.

"Sorry for the interruption, ladies and gentlemen," he says. "We have been having problems with pranksters recently…"

A flurry of voices sound down by the stage. The crowd still remain in a slight state of confusion, an incessant murmuring and whispering filling the air.

"Excuse me again. One moment," says the Deputy.

I look to see the same technician beckoning him over, accompanied by several others, as well as some members of the City Guard.

He rushes towards them, and this time I find myself drawn along too. Frankly, I can't bear it up on that stage alone anymore.

As the Deputy reaches his men, I hear the technician say: "We've traced them to the communications mainframe, sir. We think they're hybrids."

I note a quiver of rare anger rise up Deputy Burns's face.

"Send out the Stalkers," he says.

CHAPTER TWELVE

As I stand there, hovering on the edge of the stage, Deputy Burns's eyes flash back to mine.

"Ah, Brie…perhaps you should step down now," he says, quickly returning to his usual calm countenance.

I don't need to be told twice.

With a quick step, I'm off the stage and shuffling into the shadows on the other side. Around me, various technicians dart and run, and members of the City Guard tap on their forearm interfaces or talk into little microphones in their helmets.

By the little titbits I manage to pick up on, the hunt for the perpetrators of the communications hijack is getting into full swing. Clearly, these are anything but pranksters.

As I hurry further on, I hear Deputy Burns behind me, trying to continue on with the ceremony as if nothing's happened. With only a few more of us to get through, I imagine he'll be hurrying to the end as quickly as he can.

Down the short tunnel below the stage, I find Tess with the other Outer Haveners. They seem to be whispering together in a little group, speculating as to what's just happened.

"The Nameless," I hear one young man say. "Who are they?"

Several of the group shrug and shake their heads. They should be glad there are no posture police around to admonish them.

A few options are postulated as I join them and Tess brings me into the circle.

"They're probably the Fanatics," one says. "Just trying to mess with us all."

"That's dumb," counters another. "They're Disposables. Who else can they be?"

"Disposables?! That's ridiculous. They couldn't organise something like that!"

A bout of bickering ensues. It's drawn to a close by a middle-aged woman with a stocky build and stern eyes.

"Be quiet, all of you," she mutters. "You shouldn't talk about such things here. But for what it's worth…I think they're hybrids…"

Her words bring a short silence to the group.

Hybrids…that's what the technician said.

In the background, a muted applause rings out again, and we all turn to see another one of our group dropping down from the stage and coming our way.

"Jeez, that was quick," says Tess.

"This isn't going to last long," I mutter. "We

should find Sophie, get her to take us home."

"But there's a banquet later."

I shake my head.

"Somehow, I get the impression that it's going to be called off."

Less than ten minutes later, we get confirmation of exactly that. Once we've all gathered, Deputy Burns joins us from the stage once more.

"Many apologies to all of you for what happened, especially those who came after the interruption," he says. "And Brie, to be caught up in that was quite unfair. However, I have some more disappointing news. I'm afraid the banquet is to be cancelled. At this time, it isn't deemed safe…"

"Safe?" says Tess. "Why isn't it safe?"

"Well, it's just precautionary, Miss Bradbury. Whether there's a threat or not, it isn't logical to gather in large groups. However, there's no reason why your time here should be cut completely short. Your guides have been instructed to take you to their homes, where you can get a better appreciation of life here in Inner Haven."

I can see a hundred questions in the eyes of the Outer Haveners. Clearly, however, the Deputy has far more pressing things to attend to. With a courteous little nod, he thanks us again for our participation today before moving off towards the doors of the High Tower.

Tess looks at me.

"Good instincts," she says. "Did he tell you the feast would be called off?"

I shake my head.

"Like you say, just instinct."

As we wait in our little group, our guides appear one by one and begin scooping up their charges. Sophie appears a little late on the draw, arriving last of all.

"Sorry girls, it's rather busy out there. Have you been waiting long?"

"Not really," says Tess. "So, apparently we're going to your place?"

"Yes indeed. Let's get to the car, shall we?"

She begins leading us off down the street behind the towering stands and screens above. People swarm everywhere, returning to their days as the square quickly empties. By the time we reach the garage and drive back out onto the streets, the roads are predominantly clear once more.

Sticking primarily to the Spiral, we circle back out of the city, moving towards its boundary. Given her standing as an Unenhanced, Sophie and her husband occupy an apartment on the outer circle of the Spiral, close to the partition wall that cuts the city of Haven in two.

Naturally, our minds are filled with queries about what just happened. Sophie, meanwhile, appears keen to avoid the subject.

"Oh, just pranksters as Deputy Burns said," she

tells us. "It's not something to worry about."

It's obvious she's hiding something. Try as she might, she can't conceal her emotions like a Savant. The pitch of her voice, and her refusal to engage with our questions, is evidence enough that something's going on here that we're not privy to.

Soon, the car is slowing and turning into one of the many identical buildings that line the border of Inner Haven, disappearing underground. It slides into a specialised parking spot, clearly allotted for her use. When we climb out, Sophie leads us towards a lift that rises up through the centre of the building.

Up we go, shooting towards the fourth floor and stepping out into a lifeless corridor lined with doors on either side. Each one is identified by a number – 408 in Sophie's case – and opened by use of a scanner that swiftly examines Sophie's unique fingerprints and hand shape to provide us entry.

"Beats carrying a key," says Tess as we follow her inside.

The apartment carries the scent and signature of the city. In other words, it's clean, pristine, coloured in chrome silver and white and has a slight, but noticeable, aroma of chemicals.

I've noticed that it's the same just about everywhere, probably owing to the relentless efforts taken to ensure that the entire city is perpetually spotless. It's only faint, though, and is probably something that you quickly forget when you spend any time here.

Continuing her function as our tour guide, Sophie takes us on a quick circuit of the apartment. Each room is as dull as the last, lacking any life or vibrancy of any kind.

The bed, however, does look comfortable. I'll give it that at least.

The place is also equipped with some mod cons that I'd rather like back at the academy. Everything appears to be voice controlled and activated, just like the car, and exclusively triggered by Sophie's voice.

I assume her husband can also issue commands. But knowing Sophie as I now do, I can't be one hundred per cent certain.

She invites us to take a seat in the spacious and airy sitting room, and orders for the outward looking wall to turn 'semi-transparent'. Again, like with the car, the wall half fades away, providing us with a view over the city streets towards Outer Haven.

From here, it's just about possible to peek over the wall and get a feel for the more diverse architecture and structural patterns that define Outer Haven.

"Do you ever miss it?" I ask, looking towards and beyond the wall.

"Outer Haven?" asks Sophie.

"Yeah."

She delays a second before answering.

"Perhaps I would a little if I only ever stayed here," she says. "But I go there often for my work, so I suppose I have the best of both worlds." She smiles warmly. "Now, how about some drinks? Tea, coffee?"

I'm hardly a prolific drinker of either.

"Just water for me, thanks," I say.

"Got any whiskey?" asks Tess.

Clearly, her tipple with Mrs Carmichael has given her the taste.

Sophie laughs and wanders off, ignoring her.

"I was serious!" says Tess, turning to me with a frown.

I chuckle as I drop back down onto the smooth sofa, wondering how long exactly we have to be here. And why.

As Tess and I prepare to re-enter into a discussion about the day's events, Sophie sweeps back into the room, carrying a tray with flasks of water and a plate of biscuits.

Her offer to take a couple is quickly accepted by the both of us, although neither stop at just two. Biscuits are luxuries where we're from. This is not an opportunity to be missed.

For a little while, the tasty cookies are sufficient to distract us from our conversation and questioning. Perhaps that was the idea all along. As the sugar fades, however, Tess's keen mind jumps back into action.

"I didn't actually see the screen," she starts, gathering the final crumbs from the plate. "I only heard the voice – that was weird, by the way. What did the guy look like?"

She turns to Sophie, but quickly moves her eyes to me, knowing I'm more likely to answer.

"He was just a silhouette," I say. "I dunno, could have even been a woman. That modulator would change anyone's voice."

"It wasn't a woman," says Sophie, a little out of the blue.

We both turn to her.

"How do you know?"

She smiles awkwardly, and shuffles her posture a little on the sofa.

"Well...it just didn't sound like a woman, did it?" she says hurriedly.

I peer closely at her. What is she afraid of?

Suddenly, an alarm sounds on the wall. Her eyes flash and turn to it, and she darts towards the electronic interface. She presses a button, and through an intercom comes the sound of a crying baby.

"Sorry girls. That's just my son, Maddox."

"You left him here alone?" I ask.

"Oh, good God no. He's well looked after by our techno-nanny. I could leave him, but a mother's touch is always best. I won't be long."

She moves off again down the corridor, and we hear a door open and close.

"This place is sooo weird," says Tess. "They even let robots look after their kids!"

"I know. Did you hear Deputy Burns's questions for me on stage, asking if I'd like to live here? I didn't know what the hell to say."

"You did well, I thought. We all did. I dunno, though. This place might grow on you if you actually lived here. Like, if you were in Sophie's position, going both ways. Let's be honest, life isn't exactly awesome over at the academy."

"Better than here."

She shrugs.

"Maybe. I'm not going to judge it on a few hours. You heard what Sophie said. It grows on you, this place…"

"Yeah well, I'm not going to trust Sophie on this. I don't think I've ever met anyone so vapid…"

"I'd be careful what you say about my wife."

A voice, deep and firm, reverberates from the hallway behind us. We turn quickly to see a man standing at the entrance to the room, down the corridor from the front door.

He's young, perhaps Sophie's age or a little older, and has the same haircut as every other man here: short and neatly cut. The colour is jet black, though, and his eyes are piercingly dark, focused and intense.

It's the same for all the Hawks.

He takes a pace in, his eyes unblinking as they

survey us.

"You must be Sophie's husband," I say. "I didn't mean anything…"

"You meant every word, Brie," he counters.

"You know my name?"

"Of course I do," he says smoothly. "Everyone in the city knows both your names now."

He moves around the sofa, and extends a hand. We both stand quickly to our feet.

"My name's Rycard, and yes, I am Sophie's husband. Nice to meet you both."

His shake is firm and quick. After the brief introduction, he steps back and takes a seat, and we return to ours.

"So, you were at the ceremony today?" asks Tess.

Rycard leans forward and takes a flask of water, gulping down half of it before answering.

"I was on duty," he says. "I work for the City Guard."

"Oh, wow, do you get to work over in Outer Haven much?"

"Quite often, yes."

"And is that how you met Sophie?"

"No, that's not exactly how it works. She was scouted along with other *suitable* girls. We met at an official function here for Enhanced bachelors."

"Like a matchmaking ball?" I ask.

"Pretty much, yes. Perhaps you'll get to experience one soon, going by the Deputy's line of questioning."

I frown and recoil at the thought, which I only later realise is probably quite insulting. Both to him and Sophie.

"Can I deduce that you're not keen on *marrying up*," he asks wryly.

I don't answer.

"And how about you, Tess? Surely we Enhanced aren't so repulsive?"

"No, you're not repulsive at all," she says eagerly.

Jesus, Tess...the guy's wife's in the next room.

"Well, that's very nice of you to say," he says, smiling for the first time and revealing a set of straight white teeth. "Where is Sophie, by the way?"

"Oh, she's just checking on Maddox," I say.

The name of his son brightens his smile.

"I see. Well, while she's gone, if you have any questions for me, fire away. I know you're probably curious about how certain things work around here."

I look to Tess and smile. She has the same idea.

Before she can speak, however, I blurt out a single word.

"Hybrids," I say.

Rycard frowns, thin eyebrows dipping over his penetrating gaze.

"What about hybrids?" he asks.

"I heard a technician saying that the perpetrators earlier were hybrids. That they were the ones responsible. Is that true? Is that who the Nameless are?"

It's obvious that Rycard wasn't expecting such a line of questioning. He sits back and considers things a moment, his eyes turning down the corridor to check that Sophie remains with the baby.

"Yes, that's true," he says. "Hybrids are considered dangerous here. They're seen by the Court as 'anomalies' and aren't tolerated."

"But Sophie…she said yesterday that only unsanctioned hybrids are illegal. She didn't say much else, but I got the impression that other hybrids were bred, but in a controlled way."

"Impressive," says Rycard, smiling. "You have excellent intuition. There are certain types of hybrids that are actively bred for specific purposes."

"Which are?" asks Tess.

"Well, hunting *illegal* hybrids, to put it bluntly."

"Stalkers," I whisper.

"Indeed. Now where did you hear that?"

"Deputy Burns," I answer. "He told the technician to 'send out the Stalkers'."

"It's the usual response whenever the Nameless rear their heads," says Rycard coolly. "The Stalkers are our most lethal force and are ruthless hunters."

"So, the Nameless have appeared before?" I query.

He nods. "They have, but today they took it to a new level, hijacking the video feeds. It's obvious they've grown more organised and bold, and used the ceremony as an opportunity to reveal themselves to the masses…"

"Right, can we pull back a bit here," says Tess. "So, these hybrids, I assume, are mixed Enhanced? Like, if *you* married a Dasher?"

"Precisely," says Rycard. "If that happened, it's possible that my kids could have both the physical traits and genetic qualities of me and their Dasher mother. So, in that case, they would be Hawks and Dashers."

"So…Hawkers?" asks Tess.

"Actually, yes, that's exactly what they're called."

Tess grins, looking rather pleased with herself.

"And, these hybrids are considered dangerous?" I ask. "Why?"

"If you knew Savants like I did, you'd get it. They don't like anything they can't control. I mean, it's not even that hybrids are dangerous. They're just different. It's more that the Court have *made them* dangerous by outlawing them, unless they breed them themselves."

"And now they breed their own hybrid super-soldiers in order to hunt other hybrids," says Tess. "That's screwed up."

Rycard doesn't disagree.

"Anyway, how do illegal hybrids even come about?" I ask. "I mean, if relationships between different types of Enhanced are illegal, why do people take the risk?"

"Love," says Rycard quickly. "And, I suppose, lust plays its part too. Either way, these sorts of emotions are too strong to deny for some people, regardless as to whether something is illegal. I mean, over in Outer Haven, people get murdered, right?"

We nod.

"Well exactly. People know it's illegal, and they do it anyway, because of anger or passion or hate or jealously. Emotions like these can cause a lot of pain."

"And the Savants don't understand all that," I say, nodding. "They should just stop everyone feeling emotion if that's what they want…"

Rycard raises his eyebrows and purses his lips.

The room goes silent for a moment, and from down the corridor, the sound of a crying baby spreads.

"I should go check on them," says the Hawk, standing to his feet.

"Just…one more question," I say, stopping him before he can retreat.

He turns his deep eyes back down to me, and waits.

"These Nameless, these hybrids…where exactly

are they?"

Rycard looks towards the semi-tranparent wall, and sends his sharp gaze over the city. I wonder just how far he can see with those augmented eyes of his.

And as he looks, scanning the world, he answers.

"Look around you," he says quietly. "They're everywhere."

CHAPTER THIRTEEN

As Rycard disappears down the corridor, I turn to Tess and see that her eyes are tracing the Hawk's steps. She doesn't turn back to me until he's disappeared completely from view.

"Well, that was revealing," she says. "He was a little more candid than his wife, wasn't he?"

He sure was. Certainly, coming here has turned out to be more profitable than going to the banquet. I suspect that such an event would have been nothing but another opportunity to parade us in front of the members of the Court.

"And…gorgeous too," she adds with an impish smile.

"Tess…"

"Oh come on, I'm only human. It's the eyes. There's something about them that draws you in. Tell me you see it too?"

"I guess so. You've seen plenty of Hawks before, though, around Outer Haven."

"Yeah, but never up close, and I've never spoken to one. Having them look directly at you…let's just say I can see why Sophie chose him."

"I doubt it was like that," I huff. "I imagine it was *him* who chose *her*, not the other way around."

"Well, whatever. She's lucky, that's all I'm saying."

Personally, Rycard's penetrating eyes aren't what intrigue me most about him. It's his frankness, his willingness to chat openly about these hybrids and the Nameless and the Stalkers who hunt them down.

Perhaps around here they're a common topic of conversation, a current affair that the people discuss. And with him being a member of the City Guard, I guess it's probably a fairly large concern right now.

Still, I haven't heard a peep about any of this over in Outer Haven. I guess, until now, it's been kept under wraps over on this side of the wall. Now, with the cryptic words of the mystery hijacker being televised across the city, everyone's going to be talking about it.

Those words, though...I wonder what he meant.

I rack my brain and try to remember them.

He called us the oppressed. That our lives were a lie, that our freedom isn't real. And that the Fanatics aren't who we think they are.

What the hell does that all mean?

As I work to remember what else was said, I hear a door opening once more down the corridor, followed by two sets of footsteps.

I turn to see Rycard and Sophie emerge together, looking like quite the dashing couple. It looks like

Maddox has been soothed back to sleep, his cries no longer audible.

"Sorry about all that, girls," says Sophie. "But I'm glad it gave you an opportunity to meet Rycard. I hope he didn't bore you too much."

She grins, showing a bit more of her human side for the first time. I wouldn't pin her as the playful type, but I'm happy to be surprised.

"Not at all," I say. "Quite the opposite, actually."

"Well that's a rarity then," jokes Sophie again.

Rycard rolls his eyes just a little. I suspect he gets this a lot when Sophie has guests over.

"Anyway, Maddox is sleeping now, so no more distractions. How about you stay for a bit of dinner? Your passes to Inner Haven won't expire for a little while yet."

Were she to have asked about ten minutes ago, before Rycard's arrival, I'd have probably declined. Now, however, I'm only too happy to accept.

Tess also nods keenly. Her excitement at sticking around is for another reason entirely.

"Excellent," says Sophie. "I'll prepare the dining room. Rycard, fetch them some more drinks would you?"

She breezes off, leaving the three of us alone again. I find it amusing, and rather surprising, that she appears to rule the roost around here. Despite her more 'lowly' standing, in this apartment, she's the boss.

Perhaps it would be different in other households. I can't imagine a Savant ever being ordered about by an Unenhanced, for example, and many regular Enhanced would probably balk at the idea as well.

I get the impression that Rycard isn't like the rest. Other than his exceptional sight, he just seems like a regular man, one who commonly mixes with the people of Outer Haven and has gone so far as to marry one.

He's proof that the divide isn't really between the Enhanced and Unenhanced. More likely, it's between all of us and the Savants...

As ordered, he offers us a drink. I tell him that water is just fine, and grab a flask from the table. Tess once more applies for a glass of whiskey, hoping it'll work this time. Rycard appears more amenable.

"If we had some, I'd happily offer it to you. Unfortunately, we don't."

Tess crinkles her nose in disappointment.

"But we do have some apple wine, how about that?"

"Yes please!" says Tess.

It's as if a single glass of whiskey has turned her into a raving alcoholic.

In order to not feel left out, I also accept the glass.

"It's quite strong," Rycard tells us, "so go easy."

Tess appears to take the advice on board, and then goes straight ahead and guzzles down half the glass.

The effect is fairly speedy, her attention on Rycard growing steadily more uncomfortable for me to witness.

Thankfully, he doesn't appear to notice – odd to say for a man with such vision – and nor does Sophie when she returns and calls for us to follow her to the dining room.

Inside, the room is fitted with nothing but a basic table and chairs. Even the cutlery and tableware are bland. The food, however, is rather more tasty than I'm used to, owing perhaps to Sophie's culinary skills.

"Around here, not many people cook for themselves," she tells us as we eat a quite delicious stew. "Most food comes in packs that simply require heating, but I like to add my own personal touch. It's a symptom of growing up in Outer Haven, I suppose. They cook a lot more over there, darling," she adds, turning to Rycard, who attempts to look interested.

As we eat, I wait for an opportunity to further grill our hosts on what we heard today. I find it strangely odd that the subject isn't being discussed already, and that no one has yet brought it up.

Presumably, that's down to Sophie, who seems to adopt a 'head in the sand' mentality.

My curiosity, however, will not be held at bay for too long.

"Can we talk about what happened earlier?" I ask.

I assume bringing it up in a polite manner will

make Sophie more cooperative.

The table goes silent.

"Oh, you mean the prank?" asks Sophie, sipping on her wine. "What's there to talk about?"

"Well, the fact that it *wasn't* a prank," I say. "Rycard told us as much earlier."

Her eyes widen briefly, before narrowing to a threatening level, guided like a heat seeking missile at her husband. For those few moments, they're even more intense than his.

"I was just answering a few of their questions, Soph," he says. "No harm done."

"There might be harm done," says Sophie through gritted teeth. "We shouldn't be talking about this, Rycard."

"Why not?" I query.

She turns to me.

"Because the Court doesn't like rumours, Brie. I told you this yesterday. There's no surprise why you haven't heard about all this before…"

"Yeah, but now there's no hiding it. Everyone across Outer Haven will be discussing it, there's no way of getting around that now."

"She's right, Soph," says Rycard. "You can't quell curiosity…it's a powerful force."

He offers me the tiniest of winks, almost indiscernible but just about noticeable, and fills up his wife's wine glass.

"Have a little more of that, darling. It'll loosen you up a bit."

Her glare grows fiercer.

I feel I have their attention now, at least.

"So, what did the guy on the screen mean then?" I ask. "All this talk of us living a lie and being oppressed. And what else did he say…something about a reckoning."

"It's nonsense!" exclaims Sophie. "It's just fear-mongering. Clearly, my husband can't keep his mouth shut, so you'll know that these Nameless are hybrids. They're just running scared and causing a fuss, that's all."

I look to Rycard for confirmation.

"That's one way of looking at it," he mutters.

"It's the only way," says Sophie. "They're nothing but a bunch of rebels trying to destabilise things. They have no real power."

"They have *some* power," counters Rycard. "Look at what they did today."

"Oh, hijacking a video feed. It's hardly a revolution."

"It's a start," he says. "I work for the City Guard. I know that the Nameless are being treated as a serious threat. It's not quite as simple as you're making out, Sophie."

"And…this day of reckoning?" asks Tess. "What does that mean?"

This time, Rycard doesn't seem to have an answer. He shakes his head and swills on his wine.

"I honestly don't know. I suppose they have some grand plan, or something…"

"Do you think we're in danger?" I ask. Memories of the Fanatics' attack, only days before, murmur in my mind. "Will they follow in the Fanatics' footsteps?"

Rycard is quick to douse such concerns.

"I don't believe so. In fact, for my money, it's the Fanatics who are the greater threat to those in Outer Haven. The Nameless are rebelling against the Court and their doctrine. The Fanatics, however, are against the civil liberties the Unenhanced enjoy. They're warring against emotion, and see the Savants at divine figures. If there's anyone to worry about, it's them."

"But they're linked, aren't they?" comes Tess's voice. "The guy from the Nameless…didn't he say something about the Fanatics not being who we think they are?"

Again, Rycard appears a little lost on that one.

"He said that, yes. All I know is that the Fanatics are regular Unenhanced who worship the Savants. They agree that logic is the only way forward, and that emotion should be eliminated. Clearly, the attack the other day was intended to spread fear, and to get more people to side with their beliefs. It's them who concern me far more than the Nameless."

I had no idea that all this was going on beneath the

surface. This supposed utopia of Inner Haven isn't quite what is seems. If what Rycard says is true, these Nameless are everywhere, hidden in plain sight.

It's like they're the opposite of the Fanatics, Unenhanced who are rebelling against the lives and culture and freedoms of their own people. Hidden among the streets of Outer Haven, performing regular jobs and seemingly, on the surface at least, just normal citizens.

Are the Nameless the same? Are they to Inner Haven what the Fanatics are to Outer?

Unfortunately, rather than loosening her up, the apple wine seems to be having the opposite effect on Sophie. I can see her growing visibly aggravated by the conversation, something that Rycard isn't oblivious to himself.

To temper the storm, he suggests that we drop the discussion and turn our attention to other things, namely other aspects of life here in Inner Haven that might be of interest to us.

As we begin talking about how the two of them met, Sophie appears to climb back out of her shell. Tess, too, pricks up her ears and sets about learning the procedures involved in marrying up and finding a husband among the Enhanced.

Her affections for Rycard have now become abundantly clear to all, only made more pronounced by regular gulps of wine. When her glass is empty, she asks for another. Sophie and Rycard, operating on the same wavelength now, tell her they don't have any more.

The look they share suggests to me that it's a fib. And a smart one, given how Tess is acting.

The dinner concludes soon after, Sophie announcing that our passes are to expire soon and that we need to pass back across the wall. She leads us to the door, where we get the opportunity to say goodbye to Rycard.

As he shakes Tess's hand, she takes her chance to step in and give him a hug. He laughs as Sophie prises her away and leads her out of the door, saying 'come on, let's get you home', as she goes.

Standing alone with Rycard now, I thank him for his hospitality and generosity, putting emphasis on the final word. I hope he gets that I'm talking about the information he provided.

The smile on his face suggests he does.

Before he ushers me through the door, however, he inspects me a little closer. His eyes intensify and I notice his pupils, hidden within his dark brown irises, begin to dilate and expand.

They stare straight into my eyes, unblinking, in a manner that reminds me of Deputy Burns. And as he does, a little frown begins to hover.

It only lasts a moment, and then he seems to snap out of it, smiling once more.

"Have a safe journey home, Brie. I'm sure I'll see you around Outer Haven sometime."

With a little nod, he turns and shuts the door, as

his wife beckons me from down the hall.

CHAPTER FOURTEEN

The journey home is swift, my mind occupied.

We return to the self-driving car – a merciful function given the amount of apple wine Sophie has drunk – and cover the short stretch towards the western gate of the perimeter wall.

As before, the same Brute appears at the window and takes the necessary details from our guide. Confirming everything to be in order, he lets us pass, the gate once more splitting down the middle and revealing the western quarter of Outer Haven ahead.

As we re-enter the world I'm so intimate with, I look upon the streets with a slightly different eye. Partially, that is to do with the comfort of home, the feeling you get when returning to the place you know from somewhere that's so alien.

Yet it's more than that. I feel different now, a slight change in me, brought about by the events of the day and the ensuing revelations. You might say that a paranoia is burgeoning in me, a concern that this city isn't quite what it appears.

I imagine that maybe Mrs Carmichael's had it right all along. That her deep-seated wariness and distrust of Inner Haven, and the Savants in particular, isn't founded on mere bitterness, or even rumour, but a more profound knowledge of how things operate around here.

I'm so preoccupied with the thought that I hardly notice it when Tess's stomach heaves and she threatens to throw up.

"Not in here you don't!" says Sophie, calling for the car to stop.

It does so abruptly, and Tess is shunted from the vehicle and down a dirty side-street – the sort of place where an ample coating of vomit will do little to alter the décor – where she manages to regain her faculties and spare her own blushes. In the end, the alleyway is denied the contents of Tess's stomach.

As she climbs back into the car, telling us she's 'OK' in a queasy manner that's completely unconvincing, I consider that no one in Inner Haven would ever act in such a fashion.

We continue on, the neon lights brightening as we enter into the busiest district in the quarter. The streets are filled with pedestrians, a not wholly unusual thing to see at this time. And yet, their numbers are certainly more dramatic than usual, swarms of them all staring skyward with arched necks and wide, unblinking eyes.

I search for the source and quickly find it: large screens operating across the city are already re-showing footage of the ceremony. The local passion for rumour and speculation – something the Inner Haveners evidently don't share with us – will be being put into action. And no doubt both my face and Tess's will now be known from the far reaches of the north to the deep recesses of the south.

I suspect that my visage, however, will be more memorable, owing to nothing more than the fact that it was me up on stage when the interruption came. Hence, these replays will naturally feature me each time.

As such, I prime myself for a barrage of questioning as the vehicle works its way back towards the academy. When we arrive, Sophie is quick to push Tess out of the door, her stomach once more beginning to churn and lurch.

"OK girls, it was wonderful seeing you again," she says. "Don't be strangers now…"

Her voice is cut off by the door closing. Then, without delay, the car shoots off again.

I usher Tess inside, warning her as we go to sharpen up in case Mrs Carmichael is there. As with her intolerance of swearing – a great irony given her penchant for such things – our guardian has a similar dislike of seeing any of the residents of the academy drunk, a state of mind that she regularly enters.

She'll forgive the odd slip, and the occasional bout of tipsiness, but full inebriation is generally off-limits. That's a benefit that she reserves for herself alone.

When we pass the threshold – or stumble, in Tess's case – into the academy, we find that the front hall is empty. It's a blessing, and one I don't intend to waste.

With a sudden haste, I guide Tess up the winding stairs towards the second floor. As we go, I hear the distant sound of chatter coming from the common room on the ground floor. Given how that's where the only small television is, I assume everyone is in there now, glued to the screen and frantically formulating conspiracy theories.

The twisting shape of the staircase is too much for Tess's stomach, which finally gives way. With her wits hanging on by a thread, she cups her hand to her mouth to hold back the putrid tide, and I rush her along towards the communal bathroom.

It's empty. *Thank God.*

I thrust her in, and recoil as she finally lets fly, clinging to the toilet bowl for dear life.

"Jesus, Tess," I say. "You didn't have *that* much wine…"

"It's the food…" she says between heaves. "Too…rich…"

"Sure, the food…" I laugh.

The next few minutes are an unpleasant affair as I hover outside, listening to her retching and heaving beyond the door. When she's finally done, I escort her back to our room, and set about seeing her to bed.

"Brie…you're not my mum," she mutters as I make sure she brushes her teeth – that one is particularly important – and tuck her under the covers, her dress now discarded.

It seems that Sophie didn't ask for them back, suggesting we get to keep them. I make a mental note to take mine straight down to the market to sell on, peeling it off and hanging it up as carefully as I can on the end of my bed. Then, I pull on a pair of jeans, t-shirt, jumper, and jacket – clothes I feel far more comfortable in – and leave the room.

It's still quite early, so I have time to kill. I consider going down to join the others in the common room, but know that doing so will open me up to a full on interrogation. It's not something I want to deal with right now.

Instead, I move down one floor and head to Drum's room, which he shares with two others boys of similar age, Ziggy and Fred. Like Drum, they're at risk of losing their beds here. With a host of youngsters speeding towards the working age of 15, room will have to be made to accommodate them when they level up from the ground floor.

I knock on the door, and hear no response. I knock again, before opening the door to make sure they're not inside, just sleeping.

The room is empty. They must be down in the common room.

Unusual for Drum. He doesn't like crowds, let alone one filled with the nastier youngsters who comprise Brandon's posse.

Much as I'd like to catch up with him, however, I'm not willing to enter into that particular den of piranhas.

Instead, I speed my way downstairs and back towards the front door. Pulling the hood of my jacket over my head to place my face in shadow, I move back out onto the street with a mind to taking a walk. Remaining anonymous is crucial.

I start by wandering towards the large intersection to the south, where the neon advertising boards are larger and brighter, and the screens more prominently displayed.

Even before I get there, the feel of a carnival atmosphere spreads through the air, hundreds of souls loitering around across the large square as the news of the ceremony plays on loops. It's a common thing to see whenever there's any major news, people gathering here from the nearby districts to catch up and gossip.

Seeing as owning a personal television, even an old archaic set like we have at the academy, is a rarity around here, this is the easiest and best place to keep abreast of all major citywide developments.

When I reach the square, I'm greeted by the sight of my enormous face, and cringe within the shadows of my hood. Fixed to high pylons and the sides of buildings, various screens show various angles, displaying the moment the video feed was hijacked in real time.

I stand and watch, squashed among the masses, forced to endure my awkward interview again before the mystery man appears.

I look ridiculous as I muddle my way through the interview, sucking up to the residents of Inner

Haven as I tell them what an honour it is to be there.

Around me, the crowd appear to agree with me.

"She's lying, just telling them what they want to hear," one murmers grumpily.

"Sell-out," grunts another.

"Well good on her," says a woman in my defence. "I think she holds herself well. And looks beautiful."

I blush at the comment, and allow myself a little smile. A few more harsh words, however, have me moving off to a different section of the throng.

By the time I stop again, the crowd have gone silent. I watch as the screen crackles and distorts, and the mystery man appears, his ominous words once more booming out across the square.

There's a nervous energy around. Everyone listens intently. When his words begin to fade, and he's cut off, a short period of contemplation follows, before that chattering of debate once more ensues.

I listen for a while, hoping for some nugget of insight, but all I hear are wild theories and conjectures. Mostly, though, the theme is of agreement with Deputy Burns: that it was merely the work of pranksters, and nothing more.

I move off, squeezing my way past bodies and keeping my face low. One or two appear to notice me beneath my hood, but have the nous to realise I'm trying to remain incognito, and are polite enough to leave me be.

Soon, I'm leaving the square behind and stepping down quieter side roads and alleys. It's dim, the light fixings here unreliable, and yet I feel no fear or nerves.

Crime in this quarter isn't so common, especially when the streets are so busy, and only second in its safety records to the southern quarter (although, after the attack at Culture Corner, those particular stats will have been skewed). Were I to be strolling at night through the alleys of the northern quarter, I wouldn't be quite so at ease.

Still, as I wander into more idle parts, seeking the comfort of my own solitude down deserted roads, I get a sense that someone is watching me.

It's that strange sensation that people often talk about, a sort of sixth sense. An ancient instinct to avoid danger, perhaps, that emanates from our long deceased ancestors from eons ago.

It has me turning around as I walk, searching the dim passages behind me for the shape of silhouettes and glowing eyes. The few remaining people on the streets wander past, and I spy them closely, turning an accusing eye to anyone who glances in my direction.

Not one of them appears interested in my presence.

I pass it off as mere paranoia, and return to my stroll, moving off once more at a slightly brisker pace and with narrower eyes beneath my cloak. With my heart beginning to throb just a little harder in my chest, I lose my desire for solitude and work my way back towards the light.

Cutting through an alley, I see another burgeoning square await me at the end, the bustling crowd beyond a suddenly welcome sight. I move swiftly along, my stroll turning to a jog. I hear a sound behind me, and twist my neck back.

A shadow looms, right at the end of the alley, hovering under a broken light. A shiver darts up my spine, and my eyes turn back.

Too late.

I crash straight into a large garbage bin, appearing as if from nowhere. My forehead connects with its metal surface, sending my brain rocking inside my skull.

I stumble back, and slip, dropping to the floor. Scrambling in the dirt, my eyes return to the figure in the distance. He's not in the distance anymore.

He's closer now, moving towards me, hidden within a large black jacket that obscures his frame and features. I blink, and feel the first drop of rain tap on the top of my hood.

Then, building from a low wail, the sound of an alarm spreads from the square beyond. I turn my eyes back to the crowd and see them beginning to rush and disperse. Jackets are tightened up and hoods are drawn over heads, and anti-toxic umbrellas opened up as the rain begins to fall.

I swing my gaze back to the darkness, and blink as the air fills with precipitation.

The man is gone.

I let out a breath, and then, right next to me, hear a voice.

"Are you OK there?"

It makes me jump. I turn my eyes up to see an elderly man looking down at me. He holds a wide umbrella in his hand, protecting him from the rain.

"You need to get under cover," he says. "Come on, take my hand."

I nervously reach out and grab it, and he helps me to my feet.

Over in the square, I see one of the large toxic sensors changing colour from amber to red. This rain will burn skin in an instant.

The man clicks a button on his umbrella handle, and the canopy above spreads a little wider, stopping any errant drops from landing on me.

I turn back again down the alley, and see once more that it's empty. No shadow looms. No figure hovers in the darkness.

Did I just imagine it all? It has been a long day…

"Are you alright," asks the old man again. His eyes scan my forehead, and for the first time I feel the trickle of blood dribbling down the side of my nose. "That needs seeing to. What happened?"

"I slipped," I say. "It's nothing, I'm OK."

I wipe my forehead, smearing the blood, but feel only a glimmer of pain. Adrenaline can have the effect of suppressing such discomfort. Sliding my index finger over the cut, I feel that it's only small, and not deep. It probably looks worse than it is.

"Are you sure," asks the man. "It's not good to be out in this weather. Where do you live? I can help you home if you want."

"No," I say abruptly, still bubbling with suspicion. "Thank you for the offer…but it's OK. My skin's covered."

The man doesn't seem so sure.

"Really, it's no trouble. My umbrella will protect us. There's no need to damage your clothes…"

"Um…they're damaged enough as it is," I say. "Thank you anyway."

With my head still a little woozy, I step away from the stranger and head towards the square. It's deserted now, protective awnings and blinds quickly extending out from buildings, offering cover for the large screens and shop windows and anything else that might be under threat from the poisonous rain.

Many spread over the pavement, providing shelter for pedestrians caught with nowhere to go. They huddle there, looking to the skies, dark and brooding and rumbling with thunder.

Nearby, a shelter awaits for such situations, dug into the ground beneath the city streets. They litter the city, providing temporary refuge for when the acid rain falls. Down the street, I see a few people rushing towards the nearest one, disappearing through the entrance and into the shadows.

I have no interest in joining them.

Covered as I am in a thick jacket and hood, and not far from the academy, I turn on my heels and run, thrusting my exposed hands in my pockets as I go to shield my skin.

I splash through quickly forming puddles of poison, and see more people frantically search for sanctuary. Most are fully protected. Some aren't, foolish enough to leave their homes without sufficient clothing, the rain assaulting any bare areas of skin and flesh as they sprint for the nearest shelter.

I aim my sight on home, though, only a block or two away, running as fast as I can manage without falling.

And as I do, a long way away, right on the other side of the city, I hear a booming sound. Heavy, deep, shaking the concrete beneath my feet.

It's not the alarm warning of the deluge. And it's not a crack of thunder from the stormy skies.

It's something else entirely. A sound I recognise from only days before.

It can only be one thing...

The Fanatics have struck again.

CHAPTER FIFTEEN

When I arrive back at the academy, my jacket is sizzling.

I rush through the door, the night now growing late, to find the main reception hall deserted and dark, only the soft glow of a security light on the ceiling providing any illumination.

I shed my jacket and give it a quick shake, shifting any remaining droplets of acid rain. As I do, a couple make contact with the backs of my hands, bringing about an immediate sensation of pain. I'm quick to rub them dry, but the acidity of the rain is enough to leave a mark.

I make a mental note to add a fresh coating of anti-toxic wax to the coat. I haven't done so in a while – hence the smell of burning that rises from the fabric.

It was, however, sufficient enough to prevent any water from penetrating through to my under layers of clothing. I hang the jacket over on a hook in the communal closet, and note that a couple of other jackets appear to be shining wet.

I recognise them both.

One, made of black leather and capable of

repelling the most lethal of downpours, is owned by Mrs Carmichael. The other, less durable and yet with enough fabric to be made into a sizeable tent, can only belong to Drum.

Cleary, both were caught out in the rain, and both have returned recently. *Perhaps they were out together? Maybe she'd escorted him to a job interview of some kind?*

My mind, however, has no space for such queries right now. Not with everything that's gone on today. To say it's been the busiest and most intriguing of my life is quite the understatement. And now, a fresh new concern is bubbling...

Have the Fanatics set off another bomb?

With the ground floor now cleared of youngsters, I hurry towards the back of the hall and enter down a short corridor. Through a door on the left are the canteen and kitchen. To the right is the common room.

I turn right, opening the door to find the room dark and deserted. I flick on the light and move towards the old television set in the corner. It's about as old a model as you'll find in the city, nothing like the larger screens and holographic projectors the wealthier residents can afford.

I tap it on and set it to the only televised channel, which broadcasts noteworthy news and that's about all. It's more of a public service tool than anything to be used for entertainment, updating the citizens on important notices that the Council of the Unenhanced need us to hear, or notifying us of any doctrinal alterations the Consortium wish to pass down from on high.

When I tap it on, it's more in hope than expectation that there will be news about any latest attack, if that is in fact what it was. Mostly, news will filter down several hours after it occurs, with broadcasts and announcements only made when they're worthy of being seen by the masses.

My hope is slim, and quickly dashed. The screen is currently filled with nothing but re-runs of the ceremony earlier, something that I'm beginning to grow sick of already.

Once more, I have to suffer the sight of my face plastered across the enormous screens. I'm quick to turn it off, unwilling to witness my embarrassing interview all over again.

If there was an attack, I'll have to wait until tomorrow to find out.

Returning to the reception hall, I begin wearily traipsing up the spiral staircase, my head still aching from my encounter in the alley.

When I reach the second floor, I step into the vacant bathroom and take a look in the mirror. My forehead is covered in dried red blood. I look utterly grim.

I wash the blood away, before conducting a closer inspection of the cut. I'm no doctor, but it doesn't look like it needs stitches. Just a bit of medical tape should do the trick, something my guardian is sure to have.

Returning to the corridor, I set my sights towards the end. Beneath Mrs Carmichael's door, a thin sliver of light cuts through the darkness.

She's still up.

I move towards her room, passing my own on the left, and the sound of muffled voices reaches my ears.

Curious. For all her eccentricities, Mrs Carmichael hasn't been known to talk to herself. Not yet at least.

The idea of her receiving a night-time visitor is equally dubious.

I consider leaving it for now – the cut, I'm sure, will be fine if left overnight – but am drawn in by the familiar tones of the second voice in the room.

Drum?

I inch forward now, my curiosity piqued, and carefully set my ear to the door. The voices grow a little clearer, just about audible as my patron's gravelly tones creep through the wood.

"Now, Drum," I hear her say, "are we all clear? You're not to speak about what you saw to anyone."

"Yes, Mrs Carmichael."

"And particularly Brie," she adds.

My chest tightens as I hear my name.

Silence.

"Drum...promise me."

"Yes, Mrs Carmichael. I...I promise, Mrs

Carmichael."

Another delay. I little puff of smoke spreads from beneath the door, wafting up my nose.

"Good boy. Now, off you go to bed…it's getting late…"

My body reacts like a bolt.

I step back from the door, retreating as quickly and quietly as I can manage. My hand feels in the dim light for my door handle, just to the left, and I open up and slip inside.

I'm just in time. Shutting the door tight, I hear a few more muffled words beyond, growing louder as the door to Mrs Carmichael's room opens. Then, the plodding sound that always precedes Drum's presence, his heavy footfall slowly drifting by along the corridor outside the room.

I don't breathe until his footsteps have faded, descending down the staircase to the floor below.

What was that all about? I wonder. *What did Drum see?*

A coughing, spluttering sound breaks my thoughts and makes me jump for the second time that night. Behind me, over in her bed, Tess murmurs drunkenly in her sleep, her stomach still bubbling and grumbling. She groans and turns over in the pitch black, but doesn't wake.

I stand for a moment by the door, working out what to do next. My weary body and mind are now fully awake again, the mention of my name blazing my curiosity to life.

I pace towards my bed and take a seat, the wooden frame creaking a little under my weight. Snatching up my glowstick from the bedside table, I twist its end and it begins to glow, growing brighter the more I rotate.

I stop when there's enough light to see Tess from across the room, her face twitching and contorted in discomfort as she sleeps. It serves her right, really, guzzling down that wine like she did and ogling Rycard in plain sight of his wife.

Tess has a lot to learn about tact, that's for sure.

As I sit there, another waft of smoke filters up my nose. Mrs Carmichael must be on one of her chain smoking sessions in there, puffing away like it's going out of fashion. I stand and move back towards the door, leaving the glowstick on the bed, and peek my head back out into the corridor.

Her light is still on, a tobacco infused mist hanging around at the bottom of her door. Inside, I hear the faint sound of music playing, soothing tones aimed at guiding her towards her bed.

But not yet.

I make the decision, and move into the corridor and towards her room. I knock lightly, and hear the mixed confusion and concern in her voice as she answers. Anyone coming to her at this time can only be a bad thing…

"Yes, who is it?"

I answer by way of opening the door. She sits within a cloud of smoke at her desk, her fading blue eyes frowning at my interruption.

"Brie? I thought you were sleeping?"

She examines my body, and notes that I'm not wearing my nightclothes.

"Have you been out somewhere?" she questions. Then she notices the cut on my head, which she presumes must be the reason for my midnight intrusion. "What happened to you?"

The worry in her voice is immediately clear.

I instinctively raise my fingers to where her eyes sit, touching the cut. It appears to be dribbling blood again.

"Oh…it's nothing really. I just knocked my head."

"Well, that much is obvious, Brie," she says, standing from her chair. "Come in, let's take a look at that."

I move in and shut the door behind me, coughing as I do. She darts to a little window on the wall and opens it up, before tapping on an extractor fan to help suck away the smoke.

"Sorry, I wasn't expecting company at this time."

That's not strictly true. Drum was just in here…

Opening up a drawer, she extracts a little pot of antiseptic cream and some medical tape.

"Sit down here, lets get you sorted out."

As she begins mopping up the fresh flow of blood, she once more questions how the little wound was inflicted.

"Like I say, I just knocked my head," I tell her.

My words are a little short. If she can keep secrets, so can I. Although, there's nothing for me to really say on the matter anyway. Getting spooked and running into a large refuse bin is hardly an interesting story.

She doesn't push it as she continues her work. Once she's done, she retreats to her chair and pours me a little glass of whiskey. I shake my head.

"Drink it," she orders. "It'll help soothe the pain."

"It doesn't really hurt," I say.

"Well, drink it anyway. After what you've been through today, you probably need it…"

I scoop up the glass and take a sip, and an immediate sensation of burning follows in my throat.

"Jeez…what is this, acid rain!" I cough.

She laughs. "It's an acquired taste."

"You're telling me."

Some, like Tess, seem to acquire it quicker than others.

Mrs Carmichael shuffles a little deeper into her seat, and sends a quarter glass of the burning liquid down her throat with no recoil at all. Then she fills another, before zeroing in on me again.

"So, tell me about today. How was it visiting Inner Haven?"

The question is innocent, yet I know what sort of

answer she's looking for.

"Weird," I answer truthfully.

A little smile immediately creeps up her face.

"It's lifeless, colourless," I continue. "The people walk about like robots, all smiling fake smiles and being polite. They even have these *posture police* who make sure no one's adopting negative body language or expressions. Did you know about that?"

"I've heard," she says. "Nothing you're saying surprises me, Brie. I know all about Inner Haven."

"Really? How?"

She's never really told me this before. Mostly, I've always thought her bitterness has come from hearsay, and the sort of negative gossiping about Inner Haven that fills the local drinking holes she frequents.

"Oh, I've spoken with many people who have been there in my time. This line of work I'm in...I get to speak with all sorts. Outer Haven isn't short of a few who know the workings of Inner Haven. If you keep your ear to the ground, you hear things."

"You probably know a lot more than me, then. I just got a superficial look, and I didn't much like it."

"And Tess?"

I shrug. "She seemed more enamoured than me...with one thing in particular."

The look in her eye requests I elaborate.

"We met Sophie's husband, Rycard. He's a Hawk.

Tess…well, she got a bit drunk and couldn't keep her eyes off him."

"You got drunk?"

"No, not me…only Tess. We had dinner at their apartment, and she overindulged in apple wine. Don't worry, she's paying for it now, I can assure you…"

She frowns, looking less than pleased at the revelation. I wonder if I've said too much and got my best friend into trouble.

Yet, her frown appears to be based on more than just Tess's inebriation.

"I thought you were meant to be going to a banquet or something?" she queries.

"We were. It was called off after what happened."

"I see. It doesn't surprise me. The ceremony was just for show, as I told you. After the, um, *interruption*, there would be no point in carrying out the banquet. I'll bet they hated that," she says with a grin.

"The hijack?"

"Oh yes," she crackles gleefully. "Those Savants love their order. It must have been killing them that the Nameless took over their broadcast. Even *they* probably felt some anger at that…"

"It sounds like you know who they are," I say.

Her eyes round on me. Her grin drops. She scoops up her whiskey again and, with the room now mostly cleared of smoke, lights up a fresh cigarette.

It's a ploy she uses when she wants to think…or delay.

Eventually, when her answer comes, it's hardly revelatory.

"Not really. Again, just a few bits and pieces."

"Like what?" I question.

"It's not worth discussing, Brie. All I know it that they're a resistance group of some kind who are opposed to the doctrine of the Consortium. You get these sorts of rebel groups all the time. They come and go."

She returns her attention to her cigarette. She knows more than she's letting on. What she doesn't know, however, is that Rycard has already spilled the beans.

"So, you don't know that they're hybrids then?" I ask flatly.

Her old eyes flash for the tiniest of moments, before regaining their cool poise.

"I've heard that, yes," she says. "Hybrids are outlawed, so it's only logical that they'd fight the system. But…who told you that?"

"Rycard," I answer. "Sophie's husband. He's a member of the City Guard."

"A member of the City Guard? He shouldn't be so loose with his tongue…"

"I don't see why not. All this cloak and dagger stuff…it makes no sense. Why doesn't everyone know about the Nameless and who they are?"

"Because, like I say, the Savants like to keep order. They don't want people knowing about a group that could be a threat to them. After today, though, I guess there's no stopping it. There are already rumours all across the city."

"I know," I say. "I've heard them. I went for a quick walk when I got back, over to the main intersection. Most people think they're pranksters, like Deputy Burns said..."

"Most people are sheep," she returns bitterly. "They don't know how to think for themselves. I'm not sure going for a walk was a good idea though, Brie. It might be best to keep a low profile."

"Why? No one cares about me."

Her eyes turn a little shifty, and her voice deepens.

"You never know who's out there," she says. "People have agendas."

My mind turns to the shadow in the alley.

"What do you mean?"

She seems to remember herself, her face brightening again.

"Just...no, nothing. You know me, Brie...I'm in one of those moods. Just be careful, OK. Don't go out alone, especially at night."

Her words send a shiver up my spine. More questions boil to the front of my mind, but she swats them away like flies, gulping down her whiskey and stubbing out her cigarette with a fresh haste. It appears that she wants this conversation to end.

Then she turns to the little clock, ticking endlessly on the wall.

"Wow, would you look at the time. It's been a long day. Best get some sleep, hey?"

I nod, the lateness of the hour forcing me to agree. Before I leave the room, however, I pose one more question.

"Did you hear that boom earlier?" I ask. "I felt a rumble out in the streets."

"Just the storm, I'm sure," she tells me casually. Clearly, she can't have felt it like I did. "Now off you go, get some sleep. I'll check on your cut tomorrow."

I do as she says, returning to my room to find Tess now snoring loudly. It matters not.

Despite my weary limbs and tired eyes, I doubt I'll sleep much tonight.

CHAPTER SIXTEEN

The following morning reveals the truth of what I spent the night obsessing about.

I wake from a brief and broken sleep and immediately head for the common room, leaving Tess coiled up in the foetal position in her bed. Already, the academy is starting to come alive, the sound of voices spreading from the various avenues of the ground floor taken up by the youngsters.

Thankfully, I find the common room itself empty. *A few more minutes of peace before the bombardment begins...*

I flick on the television set and it gradually blooms into life. The sight that greets my eyes sends my heart pounding.

"Devastation in the eastern quarter," reads the headline at the bottom of the screen.

Behind it, an image of a flaming warehouse fills the view, the building blown apart and being hastily cleaned up by a relief team. Towards the rear, dozens of body bags are lined up, with others being removed on stretchers or added to the growing pile of dead.

A reporter stands in front of the camera, his voice

grave as he speaks.

"So far, the count of dead hasn't been determined," he says. "But it looks likely to rival the attack at Culture Corner only days ago. The warehouse behind me was operating on a night schedule, filled with innocent people just doing their jobs. Many are still being pulled from the rubble. So far, no survivors have been found."

As the man speaks, the door opens behind me and Abby comes in. She's only 8 years of age, and this sort of carnage shouldn't be witnessed by her eyes.

"Hey Brie!" she says, her innocent face lighting up. She comes clattering over to me and gives me a hug. "You were amazing yesterday!" Then her eyes flow towards the television, and her demeanour changes. "What's going on?" she asks.

"Oh, nothing interesting," I say quickly. "You should go to the canteen, Abby. Breakfast will be starting."

She frowns and squishes up her little features.

"There's been another bomb, hasn't there?"

I forget how perceptive kids can be, even though I'm only 18 myself.

I shake my head and prepare to deliver a white lie, but she continues.

"I felt it last night in my room. The ground was shaking. Did lots of people die?"

I can tell there will be no fooling her.

"Well….some," I admit, noting that she's already

seen the body bags on the screen. "But it's OK, it was right on the other side of the city. We're safe here."

"Are you sure?" she asks softly, looking for comfort.

"Of course," I say, pulling her into a hug. "You think Mrs Carmichael would let anything happen to her academy? I don't think so!"

I draw a little smile from her face and quickly reach over to turn off the TV.

"There, all gone. Now come on, let's get some food."

I stand up and lead her out of the room and into the canteen. Some of her friends are there already, giggling in their group.

"Go join your friends," I tell her.

"I'll stay with you if you want," she says.

"No…I have work I need to get on with. It's OK, go to your friends."

Her eyes scrunch up with concern as she looks at me.

"But it's not safe out there."

"Don't worry. There are Con-Cops and City Guards everywhere. Nothing's going to happen, I promise."

I've learned the word 'promise', when delivered by someone with authority, has the desired effect of settling nerves and dousing concerns. It's a trick

Mrs Carmichael taught me, herself a master at keeping the youngsters in order. More than a few times, in fact, she used that particular word to settle me down when I was a resident of the ground floor.

Thankfully, it works, and after another quick hug, Abby rushes off to eat with her friends. They huddle round her as she comes, keen to find out what we were talking about.

Sometimes, I miss the innocence of youth. Adulthood seemed to creep up on me so fast...

Once she's gone, I pop my head around the door in the kitchen to see if Drum is still on duty. With a new week beginning, it appears as though his run is up, another of the transitioners having taken on the role.

He looks at me with a bit of shock as I appear, eyes popping and his arm fixing to stone as he stirs a large pot of gruel.

"Don't mind me," I say. "Carry on."

I guess I'm going to have to get used to being looked at like that, what with my newfound celebrity status and all.

Leaving the kitchen and canteen behind, I find myself accosted by a fresh batch of youngsters pouring down the corridor to breakfast. I brace for the storm of questions and they duly oblige, a dozen voices flooding towards me at once.

"I guess you saw it all on TV?" I ask them all, referencing the previous day's events.

They all nod and chatter.

"Of course! We've seen it, like, a hundred times!"

A round of laughter follows.

"Well then," I say, "I've got nothing to add really. You saw what I saw, didn't' you?"

They appear disappointed.

"But…what else happened, away from the camera? Come on, Brie, tell us, tell us!"

"Nothing," I lie. "I just went there and came back. Now off you go to breakfast. I've got things to do."

I hear them grumble as they move down the corridor, one kid saying: "Maybe Tess will tell us."

I laugh inside at the idea. They'll be in for a rude awakening if they try to bother Tess today.

I spend the next hour attempting to gather more intel about the latest explosion. The reports on TV only give me so much, but I learn that it was a production and storage warehouse for food products that was destroyed.

It hardly makes sense. Up to this point, the Fanatics have been spraying their graffiti over art installations, primarily in the southern quarter. The attack at Culture Corner, terrible as it was, made sense: it was a public attack, an attack on art and emotion, an escalation of their war against our civil liberties.

But this? Blowing up a food warehouse over in the eastern quarter at night. It doesn't exactly fall in line with what they appear to be about.

Fresh evidence, however, points the finger

squarely at them. As the flames are extinguished and the scene investigated, the same graffiti we've seen elsewhere begins to appear, scattered over broken bits of wall. As the macabre puzzle is put back together, it becomes clear that the Fanatics were, in fact, to blame.

I guess it could have been no one else. It must simply be that their hatred of our liberties is now extending to our consumption of food. I suppose it's another expression of freedom and pleasure, creating all manner of foods that the wealthier residents enjoy. If they had it their way, we'd all be on gruel and nothing else.

As I sit and watch the latest reports, Mrs Carmichael appears through the door.

"Ah, Brie, I thought you'd be in here…"

"Have you heard about this?" I ask hurriedly.

"Yes, I have. I guess you were right last night. I wish you weren't."

She looks at me, my eyes glued to the screen.

"Now don't be getting any ideas about going over there, Brie," she says. "I know what you're thinking."

"I wasn't thinking that," I say, honestly. "I have work to do, right?"

According to my rota, today was supposed to be a clean up job at an office not far from here.

"Oh, no. I've assigned that to someone else. You and Tess should take a couple of days off, let things die down a bit. You'll only be harassed out there."

"So…stay here at the academy? I'll be harassed just as much here as anywhere. Probably more."

"Yes, well stick to your room and you'll be OK. Now let me check that cut."

She comes in and quickly inspects my wound. There's little point. It's absolutely fine. Frankly, she's been acting overly caring recently, a far cry from her usual stoic self.

Before she leaves the room, she pulls a little bag from her pocket.

"Here you go, fresh supplies," she says, handing it to me.

More pills.

Then she's off, disappearing to deliver fresh orders for the day to the youngsters, always keen to maintain a tight ship. She'll have them doing chores, running errands, learning some of the core skills that will hopefully help them find employment when they reach working age.

It'll work for some, but not for others. That's just the nature of things here.

The thought brings Drum back into my mind. As the common room begins to fill with more bodies, I take my leave without being pestered too heavily. Given what's happening on the TV, their attention is already moving off elsewhere.

I move up the first floor and back to Drum's room. When I knock this time, I receive an answer. It's not

Drum's voice that calls back, but one of his roommates.

I go in to find Fred, a small red-headed child with a face littered with freckles and a spindly frame that's in stark contrast to his oversized roommate. He's a nice kid, though, as is the third of their little crew, Ziggy, who appears to be absent.

Mrs Carmichael has always put like-minded kids together where she can. Quite what happened with Tess and me I don't know…

I quickly scan the room and see that Drum is also absent.

"He's not here," says Fred, without being prompted.

"Where is he?"

"Working. Clean up I think. Mrs Carmichael had two spots spare, she told us. Gave them to Drum and Ziggy." There's an air of resignation in his voice.

"Ah, OK," I say. "Chin up, Fred, you'll get work eventually."

He nods feebly and dips his long nose back into a book on his lap. The poor kid looks upset. His days are very much numbered here.

As I shut the door, however, I think it fortunate that Drum's got some work. And it was clearly Tess and me who made way. If I could, I'd happily sacrifice half my work if it meant Drum got to take it on.

With a smile, I return to my room to find Tess still

curled up in a mess. It's dark inside, the sharp light from the corridor cutting in across her bed.

"Oh God," she says, shielding her eyes. "Shut it…please."

I draw it to a close, nice and slow.

"I'm never drinking again," she mutters, pulling the blanket over her eyes.

"That's what they all say," comes my standard response. "You'll be happy to know that we have the day off, maybe more."

"Awesome…thank you Mrs Carmichael," she groans. "What you been doing today?"

She peeks from below her blanket, the room dim.

I consider telling her the latest news, but deduce that she's probably not in the best state to hear about it right now.

So I merely shrug and tell her nothing, before slipping onto my bed.

And set my eyes back on my parents, staring at me as a baby.

CHAPTER SEVENTEEN

The following couple of days trickle by like a slow moving stream.

Days off are rare enough. Having several in a row is unheard of, and something I'm not conditioned to. I can already feel myself getting restless.

Under strict orders from Mrs Carmichael, however, Tess and I spend our time within the academy, keeping to our room for much of it and feverishly discussing the events of the previous few days.

When I tell her about my little night-time walk after getting back from Inner Haven, she suggests that it was little more than my mind playing tricks on me.

"Brie, you were drunk, it was probably just a shadow or something."

"I wasn't drunk, Tess. That was *you*. And I think I can distinguish between a shadow and a creepy human under a coat."

"Fine. Just a Disposable then who'd come down from the northern quarter. You're asking for trouble if you wander those alleys at night."

"You should have led with that," I say. "Makes

more sense than being chased by a shadow."

"Chased? Don't be so dramatic, Brie. You just got spooked and ran into a bin. Serves you right for being such a wimp!"

Her comment warrants a pillow to the face. I just wish it was something harder.

Across the city, the latest attack sends a real shudder through the ranks of the population. A fear begins to spread, and we learn that people are beginning to stay in their homes, afraid of being caught in a blast. Mostly, it's illogical to think like that – in a city this vast, the chance of being anywhere near an attack is extremely slim – and yet that's the nature of fear.

It warps the logical mind, wipes out rational thought.

All over, reports come in that more City Guards are being spotted on patrol, and that the Con-Cops are truly out in force, casting their dead and Savant-like eyes across the city streets, vigilantly looking out for any hint of a new attack.

The number of dead from the warehouse bombing is also reported. It's the opposite picture from what we saw at Culture Corner. There, the number of dead was vastly outstripped by the number of injured. At the warehouse, however, more were killed, with only a handful of people left alive.

Across the city, the regular sound of funeral bells can be heard, a sorrowful soundtrack that fills the air each day. From early morning until late evening, the bells are regularly rung, families and friends saying goodbye to the dead, their loved ones consumed by fire at one of the many crematoriums scattered throughout Outer Haven.

Cremation is the only means of disposing of the dead now. There's no space for burials, not even for headstones. Many years ago, such customs were lost. Now, it's even rare for ashes to be kept, urns a rarity and found only in the homes of the more devout and spiritual families living here.

It's one of the many policies of the Savants that has spread among our own people. For them, the dead serve no purpose. They feel no sentimentality for those no longer able to contribute to the living world, their minds directed at nothing else but re-building the species, recolonizing the world; looking forward, not back.

Now, even Unenhanced have learned to think in the same way. When the dead are gone, they're gone. You honour them with a quick funeral, and then that's that. Life goes on.

Only, for some of us, we never got that funeral. We never got to know those we lost. Here at the orphanage, the concept of loss takes a different form. It's what binds us all together.

As our second day of captivity ensues, fresh reports tell of new waves of graffiti popping up across the city, the southern quarter in particular being besieged.

Promises of new attacks are written in bold print, warning the people to change their ways or face the consequences. A spokesman from the Council of the Unenhanced comes forward and tells us that everything is in order, and that all is being done to apprehend these Fanatics and prevent any further atrocities.

No one believes them.

That night, I go in search of Drum once more. This time I find him, hunched on his bed, covered in dust and dirt. He's alone.

"Been keeping busy?" I ask as I enter, shutting the door behind me.

Since taking over my job for the last few days, he's been almost entirely absent from the academy, returning only to sleep and eat before setting out again.

He nods wearily. A boy of his size will be expected to work hard. I'm sure his client is working him like a mule.

"I made a few mistakes," he mumbles. "Broke some furniture when I was moving it. They said they'd take it out of my pay."

"Is that why you've been working so late? To make up for it?"

He nods again. I can tell he's worried. He's had a few jobs before, but the clients are rarely satisfied. This might just be his last chance.

"I wouldn't even have this job if it wasn't for you," he says. "When Mrs Carmichael lets you out again, I'll be back here…I know it."

"You don't know that, Drum." I move in and lay an arm around his wide shoulders. "It's good that Mrs Carmichael thought of you first…and who knows, maybe I'll be stuck here a little longer."

"She only did it cos she owes me," he says.

He cuts himself off, twisting his neck to look a little away from me.

"What do you mean, owes you?" I ask.

It's unlike Drum to say such a thing. He's always been so grateful for being here, and has never spoken a word against our guardian.

"Nothing," he says, closing off.

It's not nothing. I know it's about what he saw…

"Where were you the other night?" I ask him. "When I got back from Inner Haven, you weren't here."

"Oh, yeah…how was that, by the way? I haven't seen you since then."

He's trying to change the topic. He's not usually so crafty.

"Boring," is all I say. "You were out with Mrs Carmichael weren't you?"

His bushy eyebrows lower.

"No," he says.

It's so obvious when he's lying.

"Drum, I can see right through you. I know you were out with her, because I heard you in her room.

She told you to keep quiet about what you *saw*. Don't lie to me now, Drum."

He shuffles uncomfortably, and the entire bedframe shifts a few inches across the floor.

"I, um...fine, I was with her."

He stops short, trying to give himself time to form some sort of story.

"I went to the black market with her," he says eventually, suddenly speaking with more confidence. "She needed to get some things, and asked me to go too."

"You mean, to the northern quarter?"

"Yeah, exactly. You know how she takes me with her sometimes. It's dangerous there. She likes to have a bodyguard."

Now this isn't a lie. In the past, she has been known to take Drum with her when she heads to the market. Mostly, it's where she picks up her stocks of cigarettes and alcohol, as well as the diabetes pills she gives me.

Carrying that sort of load home can make you a target for thieves, especially if you're just an old woman. And taking Drum along for the ride is a way to deter anyone from mugging her.

Personally, I've never liked it much. Drum, for all his size, is only a boy, and a timid one at that. When he goes along, it only means I have two people to worry about, rather than one.

I've never complained to her directly, though. I

mean, she's getting my medication after all, so I can't be ungrateful. I'd just prefer to go myself, to be honest, rather than putting either of them in harm's way.

"So, that's what you were talking about?" I ask him. "In her room…that's what she told you not to tell me?"

"Yeah," he says quickly. "She knows you don't approve, and told me not to tell you. That's all it was."

He's lying.

For one, he's doing that shifty-eye thing that he does when he's not telling me the truth, his murky brown eyes dancing around the room, looking at just about everything but me.

Secondly, it just doesn't make any sense. Sure, she knows I don't approve of her taking Drum, but that's never stopped her before, and it won't in the future. Frankly, she does what she deems right, and doesn't care two hoots for anyone's opinion.

"So, you two just went to the market, that's all?" I ask. "You wouldn't lie to me, would you Drum? You know you're like a brother to me, don't you?"

I lay on the sentiment nice and thick. I can see the battle raging behind his eyes.

"I'm…I'm not lying, Brie."

"Promise me."

"Promise," he mumbles, looking at his giant feet.

I have no choice but to accept it. Frankly, if it

were that important, Mrs Carmichael would surely tell me.

More to the point, I heard Drum promise to keep the secret, and don't really want to make him break it. In a way, it's nice to know that he can be so loyal to the woman who gave him sanctuary.

And on top of that, I suspect that he's only got this job right now because he's willing to prove that loyalty. If he should tell me, his last chance at keeping his spot here might well be gone.

And above all else, that's the last thing I want to see happen.

So I accept, and tell him I believe him. The relief in him is obvious, a long breath let out from his lips.

I guess, if I want to know, I'm going to have to find out another way…

CHAPTER EIGHTEEN

"I've had enough of this. I'm going out for a walk."

I've reached the end of my tether. I can only stay cooped up inside for so long.

"You can't," says Tess. "Brenda said…"

"Oh…really, you're going to use *that* line now!"

"What do you mean?"

"Well, you didn't seem to mind last week when we went down to Culture Corner. You were all for just going and *not* telling *Brenda* then…"

"That was different. We're all, you know, famous now. It might be dangerous."

"Dangerous? How? It's daylight! And since when did you care about that?"

She shrugs, all snuggled up in bed with her nose in an old book. Clearly, she's just being lazy. Unlike me, she's been thoroughly enjoying this time off.

"Look, I'm not asking for your permission, Tess. Just…cover for me if someone comes calling. Unless you wanna come too?"

I don't know why I bother asking. She looks about

as comfy as it's possible for a person to be, and outside it's bitter cold.

"I think I'll stay here," she says, to no one's surprise.

"Suit yourself."

I pull on another jumper to protect against the cold, and head downstairs to grab my jacket from the closet. Since being blasted by the acid rain several nights ago, I haven't taken a look at the damage. Other than a few extra burn marks where the anti-toxic wax had worn off, it's not too bad.

With the hall clear, I quickly slip out and pass onto the street, the surge of cold air immediately wrapping itself around me. Dragging my hood over my head to ensure I remain hidden from prying eyes, I set off on a stroll towards the market, several blocks west towards the boundary wall of the city.

The market, unlike the black market in the northern quarter, is an official place of trade, and is therefore heavily monitored. As I go, I note the additional security on the ground, and in the air, Con-Cops and City Guards stationed at populous areas, and armed security drones buzzing about in the sky.

It's all on another level from what I saw the day after the attack at Culture Corner, an impressive show of strength for sure. Yet, it begs the question of just how these Fanatics are operating under their nose.

Surely, with such a presence, a few crazed

Unenhanced should find it impossible to function? You can barely walk more than a few metres without coming under the scrutiny of some sentry or security drone, hovering above your head and scanning the world below for any hint of revolt.

It certainly makes one thing clear: these Fanatics are far more organised and dangerous than anyone gave them credit for.

And in my head, the words of the mystery man once more spread.

The Fanatics are not who you think they are...

I press on, sucking in cool air from underneath my cowl, noting how the streets have changed in my brief absence. It's not a physical change, per se, but one of atmosphere. It's as if there's a blanket over the city, trapping in the sense of fear that shivers and hovers about the streets.

People walk around with wary eyes and sunken faces, checking and re-checking anyone who appears suspicious. There's a questioning, probing ambiance, no one quite sure who might be a Fanatic or where another attack might come. Even with such security measures on show, that sense of fear remains fixed to people's hearts and souls.

And as I walk, I feel their worry seep into my own veins, the city suddenly so claustrophobic, so cloaked in dread. And with that feeling comes another.

I'm being watched again...

It's different from last time, though. The streets

are busy, the sky bright if a little misty. The neon signs glow and the holograms dance and entertain us as they jump from their projectors. It's completely unlike the dark alley, the quiet solitude.

And yet, I feel the eyes on my back, and turn to inspect my surroundings.

So many people, so many moving bodies. An impossible task to check them all.

I press on, walking a little faster, working my way towards the usually burgeoning market. Not today.

Today, it's quiet and slow, almost as many police as there are customers and merchants. A marketplace, of course, is yet another signal of our apparent greed, a place to buy all manner of goods to provide pleasure and joy.

I hadn't really thought of that. It's a prime target for the Fanatics.

I hover around the edge and don't go in, feeling stupid for forgetting to bring that blue dress to sell on. The market fills a large open square, set up with dozens of little pop-up shops that are packed and unpacked by their owners each night. Here, a lot of the food produce that they manufacture over in the eastern quarter is sold, along with the various other products deemed 'appropriate' by our masters in Inner Haven.

Unfortunately for Mrs Carmichael, cigarettes and alcohol aren't among them. With our species so under threat, products that have the capacity to kill you are generally considered to be outlawed.

Still, they clearly don't understand the human psyche. Take something away from us, and we'll continue to make it on the sly. It's the very reason why the black market continues to do such a good trade.

Quite why Mrs Carmichael gets my pills there, though, I've never worked out. Medications are readily available throughout the city at a number of places, although I suspect that they're a little more expensive when bought 'over the counter'. Buying them at the black market is probably just a money saving exercise.

As I do a quick circuit of the market, still hidden under my hood, I note a few Con-Cops looking at me in a funny way.

"You there, come here," one tells me.

I have no option but to obey.

"Why are you hiding under that hood? Take it off."

"It's cold, sir," I reply.

"Do it."

I pull back the cloak and reveal my face.

"I know you," says the man, his dull eyes moving from my chin to my forehead like a robot. "You were at the ceremony."

"Yeah…and I'm trying to keep a low profile."

He glares at me through his shark-like eyes. All Con-Cops have them, black and sleek. It's a side-effect of the therapies they go through, turning them into loyal drones with more in common with the Savants than us.

"Well, you can't go hiding your face like that," he says. "Not at a time like this. You could be mistaken for one of them."

"A Fanatic?"

"Yes. Please remove it."

"But I told you...I don't want people seeing me. I just want a quiet walk..."

"Do it," he says, cutting me off.

A breath of exasperation escapes me.

"Fine...you're the *boss*," I say sarcastically. "I bet your life was better when you were a criminal..." I add under my breath.

"What did you say?" he growls.

I roll my eyes and slide my finger across my lips.

"Nothing," I say flatly.

An ominous buzzing sound crackles down by his waist. My eyes sweep to the source and an immobiliser appears from behind his inner jacket.

"Say one more word," he warns, "and I'll zap you. I don't care who you are."

I stare right into his black eyes, open up my lips, and mouth one of the curse words that Mrs Carmichael is so keen for us to avoid.

Then I step back, smile smugly, and turn away.

A rushing noise behind me has me turning straight

back. I look down and see his arm outstretched, the immobiliser only inches from my body. There's a hand around his wrist, gripping tight. I follow it to a tall frame, and then up to a face, and see Rycard staring right at the man.

"Now, officer, let's not go causing any unnecessary problems," he says calmly, his piercing eyes cutting right into the Con-Cop's black ones.

The Con-Cop is quick to draw back his arm and fix his immobiliser to his belt.

"Sorry, sir," he says. "I am only acting under orders."

"And what orders are those?"

"To act upon anything suspicious. She was wearing a hood and acting disrespectfully."

"Hard to act respectful to a guy like you," I challenge. "For all I know, you're a murderer or a rapist."

The man doesn't respond or react. If the rumours are true, not even he'll know what he did to deserve this life of servitude. Apparently, the criminals have their memories altered to make them more subservient as part of the process.

So, he could be a murder or rapist, or he might have just stolen some food to feed his family, a family he won't remember.

I regret the comment immediately.

"Sorry," I say. "I know you're just doing your job."

The man nods but doesn't speak. Behind his eyes, I can see him searching for the truth, some fragment of his past. It's no use. There's nothing there anymore.

"Right then, all's well that ends well," says Rycard. "Come on, Brie, you should be going home. You know it's not safe around these parts."

He leads me away from the Con-Cop and over to the other side of the market. When we get there, he stops around a corner, his face crinkled into a look of admonishment.

"Brie, what are you playing at?" he asks forcefully. "Don't give me that look, I saw what you mouthed to that man. How did you think he was going to react?"

"I know…it was stupid. I just hate those guys. They're brain-dead."

"They're here to protect you, Brie. Cut them some slack."

I try to not roll my eyes. It's too hard. I fail miserably.

Rycard shakes his head at me.

"You do realise that you'd have been zapped in the back if I didn't intervene? And you know what that means?"

"They'd take me to *holding*…"

"Exactly. They'd take you to the edge of town, throw in you in a cell, and work out whether or not to let you go. I've seen people turned into Con-

Cops, or worse, for a lot less."

I huff, not believing him. I mean, I know the Consortium are strict, but seriously...

"How did you see me anyway?"

"Brie, I see everything," he answers matter-of-factly. "You need to screw your head on properly. It's dangerous around the streets now, and you don't want to draw attention to yourself by acting stupid."

"FINE! Jeez, Rycard, I get it. I'm just in a funny mood, that's all."

"Well, as long as that's all it is. Look, I need to get back on duty. Can I trust you to get back home on your own?"

I sigh and shut my eyes, take a deep breath, and tell myself not to rise to his taunt. When I open my eyes again, there's a little smile on his face.

"Good," is all he says. "I'll tell Sophie you said 'hi'."

Before I can remember how to be polite, and thank him for his intervention, he's gone.

Why is it that every time I leave the academy, something crazy happens?

Thinking it better that I just return to my room and never leave, I begin making my way back again. Hardly the most successful of walks, but at least it got me out of that damn room and away from Tess's snug smugness for a little while.

It doesn't take me too long to navigate my way home. As I go, the light starts to fade as a heavy blanket of cloud swamps the fading daylight, bringing about a premature darkness.

I make certain to check all the toxicity posts I pass to ensure that they remain a vibrant green, which they do. Still, some people consider the clouds a harbinger of an impending deluge of acid rain, so quickly retreat home.

I see a couple looking anxiously to the skies, their faces scarred and burnt from previous exposure. They must have been caught out real bad before.

Soon enough, I'm walking back down Brick Lane, the academy about half way down. The little residents and shops are closing up for the night, the darkness now bringing a deathly silence to the streets. I see a couple of the older kids from the academy step over the threshold, and make sure to hide beneath the cover of my hood again.

If I can avoid it, I'd rather Mrs Carmichael didn't know about my little prison break.

Once the coast is clear, I creep back into the academy, shed and hang my coat, and make a hasty return to the second floor by way of the winding staircase.

When I reach the long corridor, I see a little figure hovering outside my room. I take a few paces forward and the cute button nose and baby blue eyes of Abby come into view.

"Abby, what are you doing up here?" I ask her. "You know you're not meant to go above the ground floor."

"I…um nothing," she says, dipping her eyes and hurrying straight past me.

I watch her go, shuffling on short spindly legs towards the stairs and circling her way down.

Odd.

I open the door to my room, expecting to find Tess inside. She isn't, the room empty and her bed a mess. She must be in the shower, making use of all the hot water, no doubt, before anyone else can take advantage.

I shut the door and move towards my bed. Unlike Tess, I like to make my bed impeccably, rarely happy until there are no wrinkles in sight.

But there are. Towards the top, by the pillow, it's obvious the bed has been tampered with.

I step forward and pull back the blanket. And beneath it, lying on the sheet, see a letter.

In the silence of the room, I reach down and pick it up. It's an old fashioned type, not the electronic notes that are usually delivered by the drones. This one's made from paper, and can only have been hand-delivered.

My fingers curiously open it up, ripping at the edges and revealing a folded paper note within. I draw it from its sheath, and read the interior.

The first words send a strange chill down my spine.

I've been watching you, Brie.

I read on, my eyes scanning the sparse words

written in old ink.

I'd like to meet you, alone.

Come to the shelter in your district at midnight.

Don't tell anyone, not even your friend Tess.

And don't be afraid, Brie. It isn't me you need to fear.

Holding the note in my hands, I hear a footfall outside the door. Then, suddenly, it opens wide and Tess appears in her bathrobe.

"You're back," she says, drying her hair with a towel. "How was your walk?"

I don't answer.

She rounds on me.

"Are you alright? You look like you've seen a ghost?" Her eyes find the letter in my hands. "What's that?"

The words within echo in my ears.

Don't tell anyone, not even your friend Tess…

"Erm, nothing," I say, folding the letter back up and slipping it into my pocket.

She looks at me quizzically.

"Is something wrong? You're acting weird."

"No…no, of course not. I just had a run in with another Con-Cop."

"Oh God, not them. What the hell happened?"

I let out a little breath as she turns and takes a seat

on her bed. It gives me an opportunity to shift my pose and quickly shove the empty envelope beneath my blanket.

"He almost zapped me," I say. "But Rycard was there to help…"

"Rycard! You saw him again?! I knew I should have come. Right, come on, details please. Tell me all about it."

I settle more comfortably on my bed, as Tess does the same on hers.

And while my mouth begins recounting my latest run-in with the authorities, my mind begins working on something else.

Because in only a few hours, I need to sneak out once more.

Dangerous or not, I need to know who sent this letter…

CHAPTER NINETEEN

Come on Tess, fall asleep...fall asleep.

Most nights she'd have been out long ago. Early mornings and long days of hard graft will do that to a person.

Recently, however, she's turned sloth-like, keeping to her bed for the most part and only leaving it when it comes time to eat or go to the bathroom. Too many days off have turned her idle, her lie-ins growing longer and longer.

And now, it's half past eleven at night, she still she's crowing on about how much she wants to go to Inner Haven again. Really, it was my fault for mentioning Rycard. Now, she's got it in mind to go about marrying an Enhanced.

"Those eyes, Brie, those eyes. So deep and gorgeous. I wonder if we can get in touch with Sophie, maybe she can put in a good word for us, see about getting us into one of those bachelor balls for the Enhanced."

I can't help but bite.

"Um, no thanks! We have very different ideas about that place, Tess. I still can't believe you want to go back."

"Nor can I really. There's just an allure to the place that drew me in."

"Or…you're just not remembering properly because of all the apple wine you drank. Oh, and the fact that you've got a major crush on a Hawk. Who's married, in case you forgot."

"Duh. I know he's married. But I'm sure there are lots of other Hawks who aren't. Do you think I'd be suitable to marry up?"

Sheesh. Where's all this sudden interest in marriage come from?

"Tess, any man in this city would be lucky to have you," I tell her.

The room is dark, but I can imagine she's probably grinning like a Cheshire cat.

"Aw, thanks Brie. You really think?"

"Yes," I say, a little more bluntly this time. "Now stop fishing for compliments, and go to sleep!"

She sighs wistfully across the room, and I can hear her changing position, her bed creaking.

Please get to sleep…

I check my watch, clicking a button on its side to make the face glow.

Damn it. 11.36.

For a few moments the rooms goes silent. I pray for the sound of snoring.

My prayers aren't answered. Instead, Tess's voice rises into the room again, still buoyant and wide-awake. It's obvious she's not going to get to sleep for a while yet.

Forget this.

I slip out of bed and begin pulling on my winter clothes. Across the room, a side-light turns on next to Tess's bed. Her eyes glare at me.

"What are you doing?"

"Going go the common room," I tell her. "I'm gonna do some reading."

"At this time of night?"

"I'm not tired," I say, pulling on a jumper. "Don't mind me, Tess. You go back to your daydreams."

"Then why the boots?"

I shrug, thinking on the spot.

"My feet are cold…"

She watches me curiously as I leave the room, but doesn't have a chance to say anything as I pull the door shut as quietly as I can.

Outside, the corridor is dark, no sliver of light visible beneath Mrs Carmichael's door. I hurry my step downstairs to the hall, grab my jacket, and without delay creep straight back out onto the narrow confines of Brick Lane.

I check my watch. It's quarter to midnight.

Just enough time to get there.

With my hood over my head, I begin moving south, working my way through the tighter lanes that wind through this part of town. There's no one around, the streets clear and dark, all of the neon advertising displays and holograms put to bed for the night.

It's a strange contrast to the bright, multi-coloured days. So rarely have I been out at night that the city seems quite alien to me. There's a sinister, foreboding feel in the air. Every lane, every road I know so well now seems dark and dangerous.

I know I need to be extra careful. Mrs Carmichael finding out is the least of my worries. After the recent spate of attacks, and with another thought to be imminent, there's a curfew on the streets. If I should be caught, I'll find myself in *holding*. It's the last place I want to be.

I'm vigilant as I go. Occasionally, I spy Con-Cops on patrol, or have to duck under cover as a sentry drone buzzes overhead. Thankfully, the latter are easy to see coming, their lights bright in the dark and visible from a distance.

The Con-Cops, however, are more difficult to predict. Dressed in their dark costumes, they blend in well with the night, creeping about in search of stragglers.

But the shelter isn't far. And with only minutes to go before midnight, I see it awaiting me, its solid metal doors giving passage into an underground bunker. It's one of the many across the city that provides refuge from the toxic rain. When the skies are clear, however, they're almost always empty.

Nearing it now, I take a deep breath and try to

compose myself. There's a pinch of fear inside me, adrenaline pumping through my veins. And yet, beyond the nerves is something more powerful: intrigue, curiosity. I need to know who this person is.

Reaching the doors – they're always left open, in case of emergency – I twist the handle and open them wide. They're thick and heavy and low to the ground, forcing me to lower my head a little as I duck my way in.

I stop on the threshold, and look down the short flight of stairs into the darkness. I've been here several times before, caught on my way home from a job and without suitable protection from a sudden storm. I know the interior well. It's dank and smells of stale air, nothing but a cave with brick walls, a few old seats, a wooden table, and a separate bathroom for those who need to stay down here for a while.

It's also not a bad place to find a new book or two, a little stack of them on the table to help pass the time.

As I stand there, staring in, I let my voice whisper into the darkness.

"Hello? Is anyone in here?"

I hear no answer.

I ask again, and the same silence follows.

Shutting the door behind me, I creak down the old metal stairs and flick a switch at the bottom. The shelter glows a sickly shade of yellow, a single light fixed to the ceiling and casting shadows from the table and chairs.

I quickly look around and find that the place is empty.

Then, seconds later, I hear a grinding sound above, the metal door being pulled open. I freeze on the spot and watch.

Slowly, emerging from the top of the stairs, I see the shape of a man come into view. He wears dark clothing, his jacket rugged and equipped, like mine, with a hood that hovers over his head.

I feel myself stepping back a little at the sight, and wonder if I've made a terrible mistake.

"It was you," I whisper. "You're the one who's been following me?"

He doesn't advance on me. His body language isn't threatening. I watch as his hands lift up to his hood, and pull back, his face revealed to the light.

Eyes of hazel, brooding and intense, stare out from beneath low-slung eyebrows. His hair is dark brown and long enough to be wavy, a few coils hanging over his forehead, the rest swept to the back of his head and down his neck.

His features are symmetrical, handsome, his jaw stiff and tightly clenched. Above his left eye, I see a little scar, the only real blemish upon his youthful face.

And it's his age that's most striking. He's a young man, little more than a boy, perhaps about the same age as me.

Most of all, it's what helps put me at ease. Despite the penetrating nature of his gaze, there appears to be no malice in him.

As he takes a small step forward, he speaks for the first time. His voice, like his face, tells of his youth. Neither shallow nor deep, it has a quality I like.

"I'm sorry for the subterfuge, Brie," he says. "And for what happened in the alley. I only wanted to talk, as I do now. I hope you didn't hurt your head too badly?"

His eyes dart to the little bit of medical tape still attached to my forehead.

"Not at all," I say. "It's just a scratch."

His fingers feel for the scar above his left eye.

"Let's hope you're not left with one of these."

He smiles at me, his eyes brightening, and comes a little closer. Moving directly under the light above, I see his irises even more clearly now. There's a depth to them that appears in contrast to his youth.

I wonder if he's just some admirer, some opportunist. A young man who saw me on the big screen and wanted to meet me.

"You said in your letter that you've been watching me. What do you mean?"

"I'm sorry if the letter was confusing, or made you nervous. That's not my intention. When I saw you on the big screen, I knew…"

He stops short, cutting off his own voice. Then I speak again.

"Tell me who you are," I demand.

He steps a little closer. His eyes grow deeper, scanning me in an unnatural manner. I've been looked at that way before.

By Rycard.

"You're a Hawk?" I gasp.

He shakes his head.

"I'm more than just a Hawk."

And then it dawns on me. Then it becomes clear.

"A hybrid?" I whisper. "You're one of the Nameless?"

"I am," he says quietly. "I have been for many years now."

"So…you have no name?"

He smiles and shakes his head.

"That isn't what the word Nameless means. I have a name, but it wasn't the one I was born with. We take our own names on to shield our identities."

"And yours is?"

"Zander. My name's Zander."

I raise my eyes.

"You had all the names in the world to choose from and you chose Zander?" I quip.

"What's wrong with Zander?"

"I'm teasing," I tell him, feeling oddly at ease in his presence.

Still, he sees fit to present an excuse.

"Look, I was only a kid when I joined up, OK. It was the coolest name I could think of."

He steps in closer, and extends a hand. I take it, our hands wrapping up tight for a moment before being cast apart.

"A pleasure to finally meet you, Brie Melrose. You know, you're just what I expected…"

He moves back again, sinking into a dimmer quarter of the room, and pulls up a chair. I do the same, still wondering what the hell is going on.

"So, you've been with the Nameless for years?"

He nods.

"And what have I got to do with all this? Is this because I went to Inner Haven? Honestly, I don't know anything…"

"It's not about that," he cuts in. "I'm here to tell you that you're in danger, Brie. You may not be safe back at the academy."

"But I told you, I don't *know* anything."

"It's not about what you know, or don't know. It's about who you are."

"Who I am? But I'm…no one."

He shakes his head.

"No, Brie…you're not. You're so much more than you realise."

My eyes scrunch up into a ball. *Is this guy for*

real?

"I, er, I think you might have the wrong girl, Zander. I mean, I live in an orphanage and work as a labourer and cleaner. I'm hardly special."

He smiles and searches my face again.

"I respect your guardian, I really do. She's done a great job hiding you."

"Mrs Carmichael? What's she got to do with this?"

"Surely you must know? Surely you've felt *something*?"

I'm getting a little exasperated now.

"Look, you've clearly got something to tell me, so go ahead and spit it out!"

"Ah, there's that fire!" he says. "It'll serve you well. Think about it, Brie…why do you think I'm here?"

"Honestly, I have no idea. Stop playing these games and tell me!"

A little gurgle of laughter sweeps up through his throat. He's making me feel like I'm being completely obtuse. It's frankly insulting. I don't know this damn kid from Adam.

"OK," he says, his voice turning serious again. "Clearly, you're in the dark here, and that makes sense. So, what I'm going to tell you might come as a surprise…"

For God's sake…

"Just tell me!"

He fixes me with a tight stare. I return the look, watching his lips for movement. And then, out come his words. And they make no sense to me at all.

"You, Brie, are just like me," he says, leaning in. "You're a hybrid."

CHAPTER TWENTY

My laughter fills the shelter, running from one wall to the next and back again, its echo driving up the stairs and out onto the street.

Zander just sits there, waiting for me to stop. Frankly, it's probably the funniest thing I've ever heard.

Eventually, when I begin to die down, his eyes linger on me for a while, and then he says: "You done?"

"Um, for now, yeah," I say, still chuckling awkwardly. "But, just to confirm, you are a madman, yes?"

His face remains stony.

"No," he replies firmly, "I'm not a madman, Brie. What I'm telling you is the truth. I know it's hard to believe, but you *are* a hybrid."

I want to laugh again, but don't. Instead, I feel a sensation of anger climbing up from my gut. I don't like my time being wasted like this. I don't like being played the fool.

I stand up, and shake my head.

"Um, thanks for that, Zander. It was, well,

illuminating. If you are truly a part of the Nameless – which I very much doubt – then I fear for your chances against the Consortium. I'm going to be going now…"

I begin moving towards the stairs. A sweep of air flows behind me and I feel a strong hand fix to my shoulder. And then a voice in my ear: "Quiet. Don't move."

Silent as a mouse, he moves past me, his eyes staring up the stairs. A frown deepens on my forehead as I watch him, standing now in complete silence, completely rigid.

Then, his eyes change, widening slightly.

"Your laughter," he whispers. "They must have heard it. They're coming…we have to go. Now!"

"Oh come on," I say, thinking it another prank. "Who's coming exactly?"

He turns to me.

"Stalkers," he whispers.

"You mean, hybrid hunters?" I say, all too casually.

"Yes," he says, darting towards the back wall like a blur. His fingers begin moving along the brick, searching frantically, working in tandem with his keen eyes. All his movements are ferocious and hard for my eyes to see.

It's clear what else he is…he's a Dasher too.

"What are you doing?" I ask, watching him work.

"They're too close, right up on the street. We can't go out that way."

"Look, enough's enough. Joke's over, Zander."

He stops his search of the wall and turns to me, eyes screaming now.

"This is NO joke," he growls. "If they find us here, we're both dead."

"Dead...but what did I do?!"

He doesn't answer, his fingers moving quicker, eyes scanning faster. Then, suddenly, he stops, and a single brick pushes into the wall.

With a croak and a blast of dust, a small doorway appears, the brick retreating a few inches before sliding to the side and revealing a passage beyond. Of all the times I've been down here, I never knew that was there...

"Come on, Brie...we have to go!"

He reaches out to take my hand, and just as he does so, the metal doors at the top of the stairs blast open.

"Come on!"

He grabs my hand and pulls me into the darkness, pushing the door closed behind us.

"They'll have seen it. It won't take them long to figure it out," he says, pulling a torch from his jacket and shining it into the blackness.

A tunnel lights up, narrow and dripping and covered in filth.

"What is this place? Where the hell are we?!" I ask breathlessly.

"Old sewers. There's a massive network of tunnels beneath the city, from hundreds of years ago when our ancestors had their own cities here. There," he says, pointing forward as we emerge from the tunnel and into a much grander cavern. "They used to travel around their cities on underground trains. Now we use these passages to get around Outer Haven unseen."

I look to where his finger points, and see what appears to be a long, narrow building sitting on tracks. It's only a few metres tall, but dozens of metres long, covered with moss and old underground shrubbery, its sides dark with generations of accumulated dirt.

The tracks it lies on lead onwards into the darkness in both directions, the air freezing cold and filled with the clicking of strange insects and the chirping of bats.

We move hastily down into the cavern and hit the concrete earth, the tunnel back into the shelter dug into the wall and stretching away behind us. From the other end, I can hear banging.

They're smashing the door down...

Zander clearly knows it too. We reach the strange transport, built onto its tracks, and climb on. On either side are benches and seats, mouldy and eaten away by years of decay.

Through we go, up towards the far end, before

climbing through a broken door and back out into the tunnel. This one's wider than before, seemingly never-ending.

Zander begins pacing along, wrapping his arm around my waist as he goes. I can't keep up, my legs spinning as quickly as I can make them, my lungs burning as I lurch and stumble and fall into the sodden, cold earth.

He lifts me up again, his eyes now sharper than ever. Behind, more noise clatters, telling us that our pursuers have broken through now, and will be catching us up quick with their super-speed.

"We have to get topside again," says Zander fiercely. "They'll chase us down in no time like this."

I know I'm slowing him down, my capabilities only human and nothing more. *If only I was a hybrid, like he says...at least then I might be able to run faster.*

Wrapping his arm tighter around me, he sets his sights into the distance again.

"There's a route to the streets ahead," he says. "Hold on tight, and try not to drag your legs on the floor..."

Before I can ask him what he means, his body begins to grow suddenly warm and his legs begin to whirl. At first, I try to run too. Very quickly, however, I realise that I'm merely skipping on air, Zander hoisting me along as he powers into the darkness.

Around me, the wind rushes and the world turns to a blur. His torch, which was illuminating the world ahead and giving structure to the tunnel, merely becomes a white glow, with nothing but blackness around it.

I find myself struggling to breathe until, suddenly, he stops and the world comes back into view. I feel like I'm going to throw up.

"This way," he says, not giving me a second to rest or regain my faculties.

He pulls me up onto a little ledge to the side of the tunnel, and through a door. A series of rooms follow, all as overgrown and infested as the rest of this place, before another tunnel appears. This one's like the one that led from the shelter, more recently dug into the earth.

By the looks of things, the Nameless have been creating a whole load of them all over the city. I wonder how many of them are secret. I wonder whether I've given the game away, luring the Stalkers to the shelter with my stupid, loud, laughter.

The one thing I'm not wondering about now, however, is that Zander is definitely with the Nameless. And that our pursuers are definitely Stalkers. The sound of their feet, dashing along the dirt, only a little way behind us makes that clear. No one else could have kept up…

Into the new tunnel we go, this one even narrower than the first. We have to duck and stay low to clamber through, before hitting what looks like a dead end.

But it's not.

This time, Zander doesn't need to feel about for a lock, not on this side of the secret door. Pushing forward, the door opens and we pile into what seems, at first sight, to be another shelter.

When we move up another set of stairs, however, and emerge into a corridor, I realise it's just a building up on street level. We dart through another door to the left, and find ourselves in a tight alleyway.

"This way," says Zander again, guiding me down the alley and onto another street.

I look around, trying to get my bearings, but have little idea as to where we are, the darkness largely obscuring any landmarks I might recognise.

After winding down a couple of roads, Zander stops and guides his laser-focused eyes to mine.

"You need to go," he says. "I'll draw them off…they're after me, not you, and we need to keep it that way. They can't know who you are…"

"Why not?" I hear myself asking, my voice high pitched and riddled with panic.

"There's no time to explain," he says quickly. "Go back to the academy. Stay secret, stay silent. Say nothing about this to anyone."

Though the network of tight streets, voices are heard now. They're on our scent again.

"That way," points Zander. "The academy is that

way. Now run, and don't look back. GO!"

He pushes me off, forcing me to turn and run. I go, my heels kicking up grime as I launch myself at full speed away from him. And when I spare a glance back, he's gone, speeding away in the opposite direction and drawing the Stalkers along with him.

I turn again and don't stop for some time, now barely caring if a Con-Cop should catch me, or a drone spy me from up in the air. My lungs call for oxygen as I thump the ground with my heavy work boots, barely knowing where I'm going until the streets become more familiar, and I naturally gravitate back to Brick Lane.

Skipping from shadow to shadow, I finally arrive back at the academy with the night at its deepest and darkest ebb. I stop outside, and catch my breath up against a wall. My heart feels set to burst from my body. My lungs are on fire. My legs ache, trembling beneath me as they try to keep me standing.

And yet, my mind is wild and charging with a thousand questions. Questions to which I need to know the answers.

I hold myself outside under the cold night sky for a few long minutes, waiting for my heart-rate to return to normal, for my breathing to grow regular once more. Then, slowly, I creep back into the academy, stalking the place as I have so many times in recent days.

Only now, it looks different. Just like when I returned to Outer Haven from Inner Haven only days ago, and the entire place took on a different air, a different feel. I felt like something had changed. I looked upon the streets in a new light, knowing that it wasn't quite what it seemed.

And now…now I'm doing the same here. As I move up the winding stairs, I wonder what secrets this place holds too. I wonder what lies have been whispered to me throughout the years. Is the academy really what it seems?

But mostly, my mind lingers with another query. There's something else that I look upon with new eyes, with a new mind.

Myself.

Reaching the second floor, I sneak into the bathroom and flick on the light. I step in front of the mirror, holding my eyes down. And then, I raise them up and meet my gaze, and see a different face staring back.

Because if what Zander says is true, then I'm not the girl I thought I was. I'm different. Like the city, like the academy, I look at myself in a new light.

And I see a stranger staring back.

CHAPTER TWENTY ONE

I know the picture of my parents so well I could quite easily draw it from memory. The smallest of details are emblazoned across my mind, as familiar to me as the features of my own face.

I've always felt some solace in the fact that, should the picture be lost, it shall forever remain fixed in my mind. If the academy should burn down, or some cruel child see fit to take the picture from my room, I've always known that it would not deprive me of looking upon it.

That's something only time, and the fading of my memory, can take away.

Yet today, all that has begun to change. Now, the picture looks different. The one link that I have to the past, so long a mystery, has begun to grow clearer. All the theories I've come up with over the years have been swept away, replaced by a fresh suspicion.

My parents were Enhanced.

I spend the entire night looking at the picture, illuminated by my glowstick as Tess gently snores across the room. I look at it until the dawn comes and the academy rises and a new day begins to canter to life.

And all the while, my mind tumbles and flows with so many questions. Questions about them. Questions about me. Questions about the truth that has never been so fiercely sought.

But now, I will seek it out with everything I have. Now, it's the only thing on my mind.

As that day begins, I stay in my room, unwilling to leave. I make it clear to Tess that I had a bad sleep, my mood cantankerous and grouchy enough to get her to leave me alone.

For the first time, too, I'm happy for being off work, happy for the total solitude of my room. Alone, I do nothing but think, desperately hoping that Zander managed to make it past the Stalkers alive. That he's already preparing to seek me out again, to fill in the many gaps in my knowledge about who I am.

For so long I've wondered why I was abandoned. Why my parents left me here to be raised an orphan. Now a firmer picture is forming. If what Zander told me is true, then it must have been for my own safety. And, surely, they wouldn't have just left me with anyone.

They must have known Mrs Carmichael...

I think back to what Zander said.

She's done a great job hiding you...

Hiding.

Has she been doing this for my parents all along? Has she been keeping me in the dark all of my life, keeping my true identity a secret?

If they were two different types of Enhanced, then their relationship was illegal. They'd be hunted themselves, and me even more so. So they hid me, left me in the care of Mrs Carmichael, destined to live without knowledge of who they were or what they did. Truly, I don't even know if they're alive or dead. I've always considered that the latter was most likely.

I twist and turn down strange alleys in my mind, the hours of the day passing in a blur until night falls. Only then do I realise how hungry I am, my stomach churning and begging to be fed.

Needing a break, I head down to catch the tail-end of dinner, the canteen mostly cleared and only littered with a few final stragglers. One of them is Abby, her little frame crouched at a table alone, absent-mindedly swirling her spoon around her gruel as she reads an old comic book from a bygone age.

Fetching my own bowl from the kitchen, I go and join her.

"Mind if I sit?"

I seem to startle her. Her big, green eyes widen at the sight of me, broken from the spell of the comic, a story of superheroes and people with weird powers. These days, that's not such a fiction.

"Hey, Brie," she stutters. "Yeah…OK."

I sit down and note the strange awkwardness that pervades her. She needn't feel that way. I know it was her who left the letter for me from Zander. I just want to know why.

So I ask her, and she nervously recounts her tale.

"He came to me outside the academy. I was just out playing, at the end of Brick Lane. I promise I didn't go any further…"

The youngsters here aren't allowed to move beyond the confines of our narrow, busy street. Unless, of course, they're accompanied by our guardian herself.

"It's OK. I know you're a good girl. Go on, Abby."

"Um, well, I was just there, and the man came to me. He was wearing a jacket and a hood and he asked if I lived at Carmichael's. I nodded, and he asked if I knew who you were."

"And then he gave you the letter?"

"He said to put it on your bed, and to not let anyone else see. He seemed nice…and gave me some money. Did I do something wrong?"

I reach over and give her hair a little stroke.

"No, nothing wrong. You just passed on a message."

"So…do you know who he is?"

"Sort of," I tell her. "But I'm sure I'll find out more. I assume he told you not to tell anyone about this?"

She nods.

"Good. And he's right. This is our secret, OK

Abby?"

She grins a devious little look.

"OK. You can trust me, Brie."

"I know," I say, looking at the comic. "You're like my little side-kick."

Her face beams.

"Yeah, always!"

I laugh, Abby's energy and sweet disposition always helping to cheer me up when I'm having a bad day. I sit with her for a while, letting her tell me all about the comic she's reading, about the good guys and bad guys and the battles they have together.

For a while, I forget about my own struggles, looking upon her innocence with a smile on my face. Remembering what it was like when I was young and ignorant of all the terrors of this city, of this world.

Confined to this academy, she knows little of what it's truly like out there. For her sake, I hope that continues for as long as possible.

When I leave her, however, the brief period of respite ends, and my mind fills once more with the questions that won't budge. Not until they're answered.

It's the appearance of Mrs Carmichael that draws the end to dinner, coming to check up on things. She wanders in, clapping her hands and telling everyone to clear up and clear out.

As Abby scampers off, I look at the woman who raised me differently too. Everything I know, it seems, has now been cast in a new light.

"Ah, Brie," she says, coming over to me. "I wanted to have a word with you…"

There's some displeasure to her voice. *Does she know I snuck out last night?*

"Yes," I say bluntly, her presence, given the many questions in my mind, drawing some displeasure from me as well.

"Hmmmm, I heard you were in a bad mood," she remarks, noting the tone to my voice. "According to Tess you've been cranky all day. Anything the matter?"

I shrug and look away from her, my heart beginning to pace. A large part of me wants to confront her now, find out what she knows, whether she's been lying to me my entire life. But I don't, heeding Zander's words once more.

Stay secret, stay silent. Say nothing about this to anyone…

"Nothing," I mutter. "I just don't feel well."

"I see. Well a good night's sleep will see to that. I just wanted to tell you, I need to pop out this evening, so I was going to put you in charge. However, given your state, perhaps I'll ask someone else."

"No," I say quickly. "No, that's fine. I'll take care of things."

"Are you sure? You know how unruly the kids can be when trying to get them to bed."

"It's fine. I can do it. So...where are you going?"

"Nowhere interesting. There's a council meeting that I'm going to attend. It won't last too long."

"How long? When...will you be back?"

Her eyes narrow a little.

"Not late," she says. "It shouldn't go much past 11pm."

I nod silently, my mind ticking over.

"Remember, the youngsters need to be in bed no later than 9pm. Don't let them run rings round you, Brie. They respect you, so use that authority."

"I got it," I say. "Leave it with me."

She peers at me a moment longer, then appears satisfied that I can do the job.

And when she leaves me, a smile creeps up in one corner of my mouth as I stand there, now alone, in the canteen.

I don't need to ask her for answers. I don't need to confront her at all. No, I can find out what I need all on my own...

***

The corridor is silent and still. The floors below equally so. The kids put up a bit of a fight, but in the end I got them all in bed a little past nine.

Inside my room, Tess is drifting off, ignorant of

my plans and everything that's swirling in my mind. Soon enough she'll know the truth. For now, she needs to be kept in the dark.

Ahead of me, Mrs Carmichael's office awaits. I creep forward and grip the door handle, pulling down in some vague hope that she's left it unlocked.

Of course she hasn't.

The handle stops half way down, the door fastened shut. I note the time – 10.15pm - and set about fiddling with the lock, quietly unscrewing the mechanism and removing it from the door.

It's old fashioned, and easy enough to figure out, if a little time consuming. One by one, the screws come loose, and eventually I'm able to get inside and manually open the door.

I hear a little cough down the corridor and stop for a second in the shadows. The hallway is almost entirely dark as I stand there, watching as a door opens and one of the boys on our floor emerges. He turns the other way, moving towards the bathroom and disappearing inside.

I let out a long breath, open Mrs Carmichael's door, and slip inside. Then I shut it tight and wait for the boy to reappear. Only once he's safely back inside his own room do I flick on the light and begin my search.

The cluttered office lights up before me, stinking of smoke and stale air. I hastily move around to the back of the desk, a side I've never stepped foot, and take a seat in Mrs Carmichael's chair. Before I do anything else, I scan the room carefully and note everything's position.

I cannot leave a single thing out of place. I can leave no trace of my presence.

Once satisfied, I start by opening the drawers on the desk. I know Mrs Carmichael has files for each kid here, past and present, detailing where they came from, how long they've been here, their work duties and experience, and so on. When any kid leaves, she tends to continue to keep tabs on them, unable to let go as they fly the nest and strike off on their own.

She'll have a file on me, I know she will. If she knows anything more than she's letting on, then it'll be right here in this room.

I go from drawer to drawer, sliding them open, gently perusing their interiors for what I'm looking for. The three down the left of the desk hold nothing of note.

I move to the right and continue my search. This side of the desk is different. At the top is a drawer, which I open up and shut just as quickly. Nothing.

Beneath it, however, is a little door. Behind it I find the safe that Mrs Carmichael uses to store her money, opened only by knowledge of a code. A code I don't have.

The desk, it would appear, isn't going to yield what I'm looking for.

So I turn my attention elsewhere, looking to the stacks of boxes that litter the floorspace to the left and right. For someone who has to manage so many kids, Mrs Carmichael's filing system is, for want of a better word, shambolic. If she wanted, I'm sure she could afford one of the electronic tablets that would make her life so much easier.

Yet, old fashioned as she is, she prefers to keep paper records, something that's almost unheard of across the city. I've always thought that she did so, partly at least, because of her mistrust of the authorities. Paper records, after all, are physical. Electronic records aren't, and can be hacked.

Now, however, my mind grows with conviction that I was right all along. If she's been hiding information about me, and perhaps others, then surely she wouldn't want it floating around in cyber-space.

As I renew my search of the boxes, I quickly check my watch once more. 10.32. Time is ticking.

I have to act faster.

Scrambling more frantically now, I begin working my way through the boxes, uncovering promising looking files than turn out to be disappointing. Mostly, they're admin based, noting various jobs that have been completed.

Soon, my confidence is waning as quickly as the clock is ticking. One box after another leads to dead ends. Decades worth of accumulated notes that might as well be chucked out but for Mrs Carmichael's hoarding tendencies.

Then, as my hope fades, a fresh spark ignites.

Hidden towards the back of a stack of boxes, I look upon a bunch of more tidily separated files, lined up one after another. I brush away the dust and see the faded letters scribbled onto the front – *Resident Files.*

Jackpot.

I pull out the first that my fingers can grasp and check the front. *Jack Lawson.*

I slide it back in and check the one next to it. *Melanie Lester.*

Yes! They're alphabetical!

Now my heart is pumping, and my fingers are working at twice their usual pace. I flick along the list and come to the letter 'M'. Pulling each file out, one by one to check the front, I quickly find a *Phil Medvedev.*

I grab the next, expecting to see *Brie Melrose*, my eyes half a blur as they take in the name.

A frown settles over my eyes.

Emily Merchant.

Huh...

I check again. I must have missed one, must have missed my file.

No, there's nothing there. Medvedev to Merchant, with no Melrose in between.

Did she file me under 'Brie' instead?

I look to the Bs, pulling out another box that lists the first 8 letters of the alphabet. I work towards the

Bs, but again find no file with my name on it.

What's going on?

There's no file for me. No records at all. It's as if I don't even exist…

It's no use, and there's no time.

I stand from my crouched position on the floor, my back aching as I rise up to my full height and turn back to the door.

It's open.

How did I not hear her coming?

"I thought this day would come eventually," sighs Mrs Carmichael, shaking her head and looking at me through small, fading eyes.

She steps in and shuts the door, her eyes turning to the dismantled lock and screws that sit upon her desk.

"Sit down, Brie," she says. "I think it's time we talked."

CHAPTER TWENTY TWO

As I move back round toward the door and take a seat in front of her desk, she does the same, dropping into her chair behind it.

Opening up the top drawer on the left, her spindly fingers emerge with a cigarette. Lighting it up, she opens another drawer and comes up with her whiskey. And two glasses.

She fills them, and slides one over to me, despite knowing my distaste for the stuff. There's a method to her movement that suggests I'm going to need it.

I take a sip to settle my nerves, and find that the liquid doesn't burn quite as badly as last time.

An acquired taste indeed.

"I suspected you'd try to break in here tonight," she begins, a swirl of smoke drifting from her nose. "I know you better than you know yourself, Brie Melrose. You were ever so eager to know how long I'd be out."

Her choice of words is revealing. I'm sure she does know me better than I know myself...

"And you lied to me?" I ask. "You knew you'd be back earlier than 11. I guess it wouldn't be the first time," I say bitterly.

"And you believe yourself to be hard done by?" she asks. "Tell me, Brie. What's prompted all of this?"

I think again of Zander's words, warning me not to tell anyone. Much as I'd like to, however, I can't obey him. Not now. Not here.

"I know the truth," I say. "I know my parents were Enhanced. I know I'm a hybrid."

I watch closely for her reaction. She barely registers one, and that alone confirms what Zander told me.

He was telling the truth.

"How did you find out?" she asks.

"Does it mater?" I counter. "You've been lying to me my whole life…"

She shakes her head, still calm. As she said, she knew this day was coming. She's spent my entire life preparing for it.

Her croaky voice continues to break into the silence, smoke spilling from her lips and nose as she speaks. It's the one thing that gives away the nerves inside her: her proclivity for smoking a little faster when under duress.

And as well as she knows me, I know her too. I can see through her external poise to the growing turmoil within.

"There's a difference, Brie, between lying and withholding the truth. I have been doing the latter, and I've been doing it for your protection."

"My protection? You don't think I can handle the truth?"

"It's not about handling the truth. It's about staying safe. I've only wanted to keep you from harm, that's all. The truth was only ever going to bring you pain."

"It's my pain, *Brenda*," I say. Her eyes widen a little at the use of her first name. "It's not yours to keep. And neither is the truth. Now tell me...tell me everything."

My words fade into silence. A drawn out breath escapes her. I note the slightest tremble of her fingers as she raises her glass to her lips, and sinks its entire contents.

Mine remains before me, untouched but for a sip. I merely stare at her, awaiting her voice, my heart growing oddly steady as she prepares to speak.

"I knew your father," she says finally. "He was a member of the City Guard, and would often patrol the streets around here. He was kind and friendly to the people, and was nice to the kids here when they were out on the streets. They were fascinated by him, as you would be...given his gifts. He was a Hawk. His eyes...they were just like yours."

I feel a swell of sadness grip at me as she speaks, his eyes appearing before mine, as they so often do.

"And...my mother?" I whisper.

She shakes her head.

"I knew nothing of her. All I know is that she was from Inner Haven too, and that their relationship was illegal. Your father grew more interested in the academy as time went by, asking so many questions. I got the feeling he was trying to work us out, Derek and myself. Figure out if we were good people, good guardians."

She takes another swig of whiskey, her eyes growing moist with a glistening of tears.

"One day, he came to us. He was…distressed. He told us about his relationship with your mother, something that they'd been trying to keep a secret. But…they'd been discovered, and had no choice. They had to give you up, Brie. So he brought you to me."

Now it's my eyes that grow wet. It's been so many years since I've shed a tear, my heart growing cold to such emotion. Not today. Today I feel my cheeks grow warm, salty brine silently sliding towards the corners of my mouth.

"Your parents knew that you'd be hunted down if they discovered you. The last thing they wanted was to give you up, you must understand that. Your father made me promise to keep the truth from you…until you came calling for it. He knew, like I did, they this day would come."

Now I can't hold back. I reach for my whiskey and let the burning liquid fizzle in my throat, distracting me from my grief, if only for a moment.

"What happened to them?" I whisper. "After they gave me up?"

"I don't know for sure," she says. "I…I never saw

him again. But…"

"You think they're dead?"

She nods silently.

"And the picture?" I sniff.

"Your father brought it with him. He wanted you to at least know what they looked like, if not who they were. It's all he could do. Anything else could have put you in danger."

I take another sip of whiskey, and sniff away a few tears, wiping my cheeks with my sleeve. Mrs Carmichael reaches forward and refills my glass. I don't object.

Then my mind turns backwards, and I think of Mrs Carmichael's dislike for Inner Haven, her hatred of the doctrine sent down by the Court and Consortium. Such things must be rooted in what happened to my parents, the fate they suffered because their relationship was deemed illegal. We here in Outer Haven think we're hard done by, but truly the Enhanced have it worse.

They're little more than slaves to their masters, so entrenched in *their* world that they no longer know the benefits of freedom that we continue to enjoy. After so many years of indoctrination, they've learned to accept their place, living in an emotionless world of the Savants' design.

My parents broke those rules, and they suffered for it. It breaks my heart to think of their pain at giving me up, knowing what I'd become should I take on their gifts.

But I haven't. All my life I've been normal, human, just a regular Unenhanced living a regular life.

I look to Mrs Carmichael, sitting silently and watching my mind tick over. A question bubbles to my lips, but before it can fall, a realisation does so first.

"The pills," I whisper. "I…I don't have diabetes, do I?"

My guardian continues to look at me, her eyes sunken and tired and old. Her head shakes.

"The black market," I continue. "You go there to get pills to suppress my gifts, to keep me human? You've been doing it all my life…"

"I had to," she says, her voice a croaky whisper. "I had to keep your abilities from emerging, I promised your father I would."

"And…is that what Drum saw," I ask. "I heard you in here the other night, telling him to keep quiet. You'd taken him to the black market, hadn't you…and he'd seen something he shouldn't have."

Her frail fingers linger constantly around her mouth now, her lungs filling and emptying of smoke almost every other breath.

"I suppose you might as well know now," she says. "I've been getting your medication from the Nameless for years…they manufacture it to help keep people safe, and to shield their gifts from the Consortium. Drum saw me with them. I doubt he truly knew what was going on, but I didn't want him saying anything. I never wanted you to find out about this…"

"But I had to eventually," I say. "What would you have done when I left this place and moved elsewhere, or found a man to marry?"

"I guess I thought I'd keep giving you the pills. Keep track of you. I want better for you than what happened to your parents, Brie. If you go off your medication, your powers will manifest, and you'll be found out. It might take a month or a year or more…but they'll find you eventually."

She looks at me more closely again, the cogs ticking behind her eyes.

"Unless," she continues, "you've already been found. Who was it that told you, Brie. Tell me."

"I don't know," I say. "Just a boy…one of the Nameless. He'd seen me at the ceremony. He knew who I was…"

"But how? I've kept you hidden from them. They never knew who the pills were for…"

"I don't know. We didn't get to speak for long. We were…interrupted."

She grits her teeth and narrows her eyes.

"Interrupted?"

"Stalkers," I say, almost guiltily. "They found us…but he got us away from them."

"Oh, Brie! That's exactly why I didn't want you going to that ceremony. I knew something was going to happen. I knew it would be a slippery slope…"

"Something did happen," I cut in. "I found out the *truth*. And I'm happy for it."

"You shouldn't be. I can already see where this is going…you're already falling deeper. You should forget all of this, Brie. Stick with your medication, forget who you are, and get on with your life. It's what your parents would have wanted."

"No," I say quickly. "No…if my parents were killed for falling in love, then that's not something I can live with. I can't just sit back and do nothing…"

Mrs Carmichael drops her head, her posture deflating like a popped balloon. She looks older than she ever has before, more weary. As if she's been trying to hold back this tide for so many years, trying to prevent the dam from bursting.

But she can't stay the flood forever. Something has changed in me now. There is no going back.

And she knows it.

"You're going to try to find them, aren't you?" she whispers, defeated. "The Nameless…"

Her murky eyes lift again, resignation inside them. It's a look of failure.

She hasn't failed.

I stand, and move around the desk, and lean down in front of her. I take a grip of her fingers, wrinkled and sallow from her incessant smoking, and cup them warmly between my palms.

"I love you, Brenda Carmichael," I tell her. "I'll

never forget what you've done for me. And I don't blame you for withholding the truth. You did what my father asked you to do, and you did what you thought was right. But I can't go on as normal, as if nothing's happened. These last few days, they've opened my eyes, my mind. I have to do my part. You had no choice, and neither do I."

She smiles weakly, and a trickle of tears work their way down the network of wrinkles across her cheeks.

"What will you do?" she asks me weakly.

"I...I don't know exactly. I need to find this boy again. There's still so much more I have to learn. After that...I guess only time will tell."

Her thin lips work into a smile, and she pulls me into a hug, her bony arms coiling round me and gripping me tighter than ever.

"The northern quarter," she whispers into my ear. "Go to the black market. Ask for Walter and tell him I sent you. If this boy is truly a member of the Nameless, he'll help you find him."

I lean back, and see the fresh surge of conviction spread across her face.

"You're helping me?"

"Sweet girl," she says, laying her withered hand on my cheek, "I know you're going to go anyway. The seed has been planted. There's no stopping that now. So I will do what I can to help, and I want to make sure that this boy is who he says he is. Walter will know. Go to him, and he'll help you find the truth."

She reaches into her a drawer in her desk, and pulls out a pair of glasses. They're simple, built from a thin, silver frame and with a light blue shade to their lenses. She hands them to me.

"Take these," she says. "The black market moves around to avoid detection. Go to district 5 in the centre of the northern quarter, and put these on. They'll reveal the markings...follow them and you'll get to the market."

I take the glasses from her, and slip them into my pocket.

"I...I don't know what to say."

"There's nothing else to say," she says. "Except that...your parents would have been so proud of you. Of the young woman you've become," she croaks. "As I am."

I smile and pull her into another hug, a large part of me not wanting to let go. Wanting instead to take her advice, to forget all of this, to carry on living in ignorance of the truth. But I can't now. I have no choice.

And as I grip tight to her old body, I whisper into her ear again.

"You *are* my parent," I tell her. "That will never change."

I release her, and drift away. And with a final look, gaze upon this woman who raised me as her own. Kept me secret and safe. Fulfilled her promise to my father that she made so many years ago.

But now, she's done her part. She's done everything she could to allow me to live a normal life. To stay safe from those who'd try to take me away.

Those days, however, are done.

And now, my world is set to open in ways I could never have imagined.

CHAPTER TWENTY THREE

I pack in secret. Essentials, nothing more. A few bits of clothing, toothbrush, the glasses that Mrs Carmichael gave me. And, of course, the picture of my parents, folded up as neatly as possible and deposited in the inside pocket of my jacket.

I don't take much, partly because I don't *have* much to take, and partly because, as far as I know it, I might well be right back here later tonight. My path ahead is far from clear. Truly, I'm running on nothing but instinct right now.

But there's a drive in me to act, and not to just wait around here for Zander to rear his head. It's been less that two days since we met, and yet I feel an urgency to take the next step. For my entire life, I've been consigned to the shadows, kept in the dark.

No longer. I'm seeking the light myself.

My guardian's suspicions also need to be considered. Right now, I don't really know anything about Zander other than what he told me, and having complete trust in strangers has always been something that Mrs Carmichael has warned against.

Seeing her contact, Walter, will help me confirm his story and association with the Nameless. It's only prudent that I act upon her advice, given what she's done for me.

I decide not to tell Tess. Confronting Mrs Carmichael and learning the truth was one thing. Immediately relaying it all to Tess would be another. Right now, I need to strike out with no distractions at all, and involving my best friend is only going to complicate things.

The same goes for Drum. I console myself with the thought that, should I be gone for long, he'll be able to take some of the work left in my absence. But, like me, the last thing he needs are any distractions of his own.

I act as normally as I can manage that day, sticking to my room for the most part. Only when Tess has left the room to fetch some food am I able to prepare my departure, hastily packing away my things before hiding the bag under my bed should she return.

The removal of my parents' picture will no doubt cause some confusion in her when she notices it's no longer attached to the wall. By that point, however, I'll be long gone, deep in the recesses of the northern quarter in my continued hunt for the truth.

I suppose I've always been a curious girl, although never to this extent. For years I've found myself wondering about a great many things about Inner Haven, the nature of the Savants, the truth about exactly what's going on beyond the borders of this city.

Now, however, that curiosity has reached fever pitch, my own existence, my own past, thrust right into the centre of it all. It's like a fire has been lit within me, the flames stoked and turned wild. My yearning for the truth – the full truth – is raging inside, a thirst only quenchable by venturing to some dangerous places.

And the northern quarter is most certainly that.

As the afternoon shifts along, and Tess once more disappears down into the common room, I decide to take my leave. Slipping my bag onto my back, I hastily wind down the stairs and head for the communal closet. I fetch my jacket, wrap myself up, and head for the building's exit.

With a final look upon the academy, I take a breath and disappear onto Brick Lane, quickly swallowed up by the stream of people working their way up and down the narrow street.

I don't look back as I work my way north, seeking the nearest boarding point for the Conveyor Line. There's one handily situated at the top end of Brick Lane, a cluster of people queuing up to board as the standing transport slows at a certain juncture, allowing them to step on.

I join the back, and am quickly climbing aboard myself, heading off in a northerly direction. With the afternoon quickly subsiding, the streets begin to grow a little clearer as I journey on.

The boundaries separating the four quarters of Outer Haven aren't immediately discernible. There's no wall, for example, like the one separating us from Inner Haven. There are no checkpoints to clarify which part of the city you're in.

Instead, there's a distinct feel, or flavour, to each area. The south is mostly determined by its art and culture, by its relative wealth compared to the other quarters.

The west, where I reside, is the busiest residential area, the streets winding and bustling, filled with little trade shops and markets, and larger squares where the neon lights and advertising boards and giant holograms are at their most prominent.

The east, where the shape of the earth rises a little higher, is known for its manufacturing and industry, large swathes of it given over to the factories and warehouses that chug away, night and day, to create the food and other commodities that the residents of the city need.

Then there's the north, characterised by its destitution and poverty, itself divided by its various districts. In the southern part of the quarter it's largely residential, linking seamlessly with the tower blocks and other urban dwellings that dominate the western quarter. There, it's relatively safe, if a little grim and dank and dirty, the neon glow of the advertising growing sparse and dim.

Go further north, however, and you'll find yourself in an old industrial area, no longer in operation and long since abandoned. Up there, where the Disposables dwell, law and order barely functions, the place mostly forgotten and avoided by the residents of the city.

It's a place I've never been, where remnants and relics of the old world still remain, the skeletons of ancient buildings still littering the cracked and broken streets. Venture there, and you'd better have a good reason. It isn't a place for the faint of heart.

The change in the light grows apparent as I go, cruising along the Conveyor Line and into the southern districts of the north. As the daylight starts to fade, bringing the first signs of night, so do the advertising boards, thought to be useless around here. After all, no one has the money to buy the products they're touting.

The multi-coloured drench that I'm so used to becomes non-existent, replaced by a dark grey palette that brings with it a threatening and ominous feel. A menacing atmosphere that only grows more foreboding the further north I travel.

Soon, however, the Conveyor Line swerves off eastwards, reaching its most northerly point. I step off, and look upon older lines and junctions that once spread right to the northernmost part of Outer Haven.

No more.

Now, they're nothing but relics themselves, left to wither and die in much the same manner as the streets and districts they used to service.

I have no choice but to continue on foot, working my way through the gritty streets and towards district 5. As far as I know it, the black market remains hidden to those who don't know about it, a necessary means to keep it concealed from the authorities.

Only from district 5 can you find the markings that will take you there, hidden in plain sight and only visible through the special lenses Mrs Carmichael provided.

The light continues to weaken as I go, the sun giving way to the moon and the grey sky to a black blanket of night. Around here, the streetlights are poorly maintained too, some flickering or only emitting a faint glow, others not working at all.

The only saving grace appears to be the lack of cloud cover. Above, the night is clear, the stars and moon visible and providing some illumination on the streets.

Unfortunately, the market only operates after hours, necessitating this night-time venture. Still, the streets aren't entirely absent of life, people lingering here and there, some of them perhaps searching, as I am, for the latest location of the market.

Given my lack of knowledge of the area, I have a little trouble knowing if and when I'm actually in district 5. Asking a few of the local residents turns out to be fruitless, no one willing to offer any aid to a girl like me.

Seeing this place for what it really is makes me value the work and care of Mrs Carmichael even more. And yet, so many who come through the academy will still end up around these parts, spat out here to the cesspool of the city to scratch a living in the dirt.

I wonder if I pass anyone I might have known from the past, or anyone who came before me. Over my lifetime at Carmichael's, many have come and gone, some going on to live normal lives, others cast adrift when they're unable to support themselves.

I think again of Drum, still so close to that particular precipice. Despite his size and strength, I doubt he'd survive long out here.

Given the looks I'm getting, I might not survive long either. As I continue to press on, asking passers by for my location, I get the distinct impression that I'm not wanted here. It's as though they can tell I'm an outsider, drawn here for a specific purpose. I guess they have reason to be distrustful, given the treatment they've endured.

Still, I finally get a straight answer from an old woman, shuffling along the street, her back curved and hunched over.

"Yes…district 5," she mutters without looking up, the warped shape of her back making such a thing impossible.

"Thank you," I tell her as she waddles onwards in the shadows.

I swing the bag from my back and open it up, retrieving the glasses within. Setting them to my nose, the blue lenses alter the colour of my surroundings, lightening them with a sapphire tint.

And in the distance, in an empty little square nestled between derelict buildings, I see a little pattern light up brighter than everything else around it.

I rush on, growing closer, and note that the pattern is a symbol, a circular spiral similar to the badge of the city officials, or the shape of the streets of Inner Haven itself. I would consider it curious if I had any inclination to ponder it. But I don't.

Instead, I see that the spiral shape ends in a little arrow, right in the middle of the coil, pointing off towards the east. I follow it down a narrow street, rushing towards the sight of another glowing pattern at the end. This time, the same signal appears, only with its arrows pointing north.

I further series of markings draws me further into the depths of the northern quarter, my pace growing as I follow the trail in search of the market. Soon enough, I'm being lured into eerily silent places, the old tower blocks creating menacing shadows that blot out the moonlight.

Then, I reach a final marking, this one different from the others. No arrow exists in the middle, no further directions given. I remove the glasses, casting the world back into its bitter shades of grey and black, and look upon a door.

Pressing forward, it creaks open, revealing a passageway into a low, narrow building. I move down it, and from the distant shadows a looming figure appears.

He eyes me suspiciously as I near him, dressed in the darkest of blacks and the size of a Brute. From his barrel chest, a booming voice growls.

"What's your business here?" he asks me.

The voice sends shivers through me, such is its power, bouncing around the walls of the narrow passageway.

"I'm here to visit the black market," I say, showing my glasses. "I've been following the signs."

My explanation seems enough for him. He nods and steps to one side, then reaches out and pulls a door open. Behind, I see the form of a large open space appear, a high ceiling made from broken glass and a skeleton of metal, casting the place in a fresh dose of moonlight.

I wander in, and send my eyes over what appears to be an old train station, right in the north of the oldest part of the city. A place that once thrived with life, now overgrown and thriving for a different reason.

I see various stalls set up under the dim light, little different from those in the official markets where I reside. People in dark cloaks and jackets creep about, buying the products deemed illegal by the Court. Many, I know, will live in more pleasant areas of the city, coming here like Mrs Carmichael to satisfy their vices. Despite the unpleasantness of getting here, I feel relieved to be amongst people again, my soaring heart rate beginning to settle as I step in and begin my new search.

This time, it's the man named Walter that I'm looking for.

I assume that this particular search will be easier. Casting my eyes over the stalls, set up in the various nooks and crannies of the old station, I look for one selling drugs and medication. Walter, it would appear, is a proprietor of such goods, an underground apothecary who's clearly in contact with the Nameless, if not a member himself.

Finding him, however, isn't quite as simple as I'd hoped. When I offer his name, either to browsers or merchants, I'm greeted with a mixture of shrugging shoulders, shaking heads, and narrowing eyes. Many appear to be unaware of who he is. Others, however, merely appear suspicious of my asking, or unwilling to pass on such details.

It's as if they consider me untrustworthy, perhaps even a spy for the council. Or worse, the Court. A girl of my age, wandering around down here when I clearly don't know the area, is cause to be sceptical. I guess I can't blame anyone for that, particularly given the Savants' treatment of the Nameless and those who associate with them.

Still, I continue my search with a little more force, and eventually manage to find someone willing to help. An old shopkeeper, nestled in a dark corner, selling the whiskey Mrs Carmichael loves so dearly. He eyes me from beneath bushy black brows, maintaining a guarded gaze until the name of my guardian drops from my mouth.

"You're one of Brenda's kids?" he asks, eyes brightening a little.

I nod hastily.

"I assume she gets her whiskey from you?"

"Oh…yes indeed. She's one of my top customers. Now, how can I help you, young lady?"

I let out a breath of relief, his visage growing suddenly more welcoming. Around here, it's all about who you know. Clearly.

"I'm looking for a man named Walter," I say. "He sells medications…drugs." I lower my voice and lean in. "I understand he's with the *Nameless*?"

The man mimics my movements, leaning in too, lowering his tone.

"Now what do you want with a man like that?"

"Information," I say. "I just want to talk."

"And Brenda sent you here?"

I nod. It's half true, at least.

"Alright. I'll help you."

He turns his eyes to the rear of the station, where an old train sits on tracks. Outside, I note the presence of another guard, blocking a doorway in.

"That's where you wanna be," he tells me. "Walter operates off the main market at the back of that train. Don't mention I told you…"

"I won't," I say. "And thank you."

He nods and continues to busy himself with his stocks, before turning to another customer who slips in from the crowd.

As I move off to the rear of the station, I find the

new guard eyeing me closely, just like the last. This one, however, isn't particularly large. Instead, his piercing gaze, eyes like lights and visible from a distance, suggest he's a Hawk. And quite possibly a hybrid himself.

To his side, the shape of a large gun, hidden beneath his cloak, makes it clear he means business. I see his hands reach down and take a firmer handle of the weapon as I approach.

"I'm here to see Walter," I say confidently.

"He's busy," comes a quick, terse reply.

"No," comes mine. His eyes narrow. "I've come too far today to be turned away. Tell him Brenda Carmichael sent me. Tell him it's important."

He considers me a second.

"Wait here."

Turning, he opens up the door and disappears inside. A few moments later, the door opens again, and he nods me in. I enter, and look down the gloomy interior, a broken down wreck of a train, similar to the one I passed through beneath the surface of the city two nights ago.

At the end, a desk awaits, a single lamp glowing upon it. And behind it, a middle-aged, balding man with sleek eyes and an oddly friendly countenance. His face appears to carry a natural smile that seems at odds with his surroundings, and the tense nature of the situation.

"You're here on Brenda's behalf?" he asks, his voice bounding towards me from the other end of the train. "Come here, girl…step into the light."

I begin moving towards him as the guard re-assumes his vigil outside.

He watches me come, eyes scanning me with interest. Then, they open a little, and he begins nodding, seemingly haven drawn some conclusion from my appearance.

"So it's you, is it," he says. "You're the one Brenda's been buying my medication for…"

It's not a question, but a statement.

Still I answer with a nod.

"Curious that you're here. She only came a few days ago to refill her stocks. I sense this is about something else. The truth, perhaps. Is that what you're here for?"

"I'm here for information," I say.

"And your name?"

I hesitate for a second. He laughs, a throaty gurgle emptying into the room.

"You can trust me, girl. We're on the same side."

"The Nameless?" I ask. "Are you with them?"

"I fear you don't know how this works," comes his swift voice. "I asked you a question. It's courtesy to answer before asking your own."

"I…I'm sorry. My name's Brie."

A new smile flourishes on his crinkly face.

"Yes, I know," he says. "Even in these dark

corners, we saw the footage from the ceremony the other day. Merely tying your hair back isn't enough to shield your look."

"I'm not trying to shield it," I say. "Not to you."

"Good. Honesty is something I appreciate. Now, to your question…yes, I am with the Nameless. That is no particular secret to the people around here."

"So you're a…a hybrid?"

"Oh no, just a man," he says. "The Nameless are not only hybrids. We are comprised of people from all walks of life. My path brought me here long ago. Now, I help manufacture and sell the drugs that offer people sanctuary from the Consortium's iron rule. People like you, Brie. And yet…here you are. What is it you want to know from me?"

"Like I say, just information. I'm looking for someone…one of your people. He came to me two nights ago, set me on this track. It was him who told me what I am. And I need to know more."

"I see. And Brenda truly knows you're here?" he questions.

I pull out the glasses from my bag and show them to him.

"Yes, she gave me these, told me to follow the markings and find you. She trusts you, clearly, but not this boy. She wants to know if he's with you…"

"And his name?"

I slip the glasses back into the bag.

"Zander," I say.

Walter peers at me again, before a frown settles over his eyes. Then, as he's about to speak, the door thrusts open behind me, and I turn to see the guard pace aboard the derelict train.

His piercing eyes are wide in the shadows, his hands now primed around his pulse rifle.

"Sir, we have to go..." he says fiercely.

"What's going on?" asks Walter, standing.

The guard doesn't need to answer.

Because, right on the other side of the station, a clattering sound answers for him.

Gunfire.

CHAPTER TWENTY FOUR

Walter shoots down the train and to the exit, dragging me along with him.

"We have to get you out of here, Brie. This isn't safe. You should never have come."

"What's going on?" I ask, a panic setting in me.

"They've tracked the market. No one here is safe."

Drawing a handgun from his jacket, he stops at the doorway alongside his bodyguard. The Hawk stands on the threshold, guiding his gaze to the space beyond, hastily analysing our escape routes.

Standing behind them both, I get a few glimpses into the distance, the cavernous space now echoing with a mixture of gunfire and screaming and the hurrying of escaping bodies.

The dim hall lights occasionally with flashes as the weapons sing their song, some chattering as they spew lead bullets, others pulsing as red and blue blasts of energy rip from their rifles. A mixture of the old and the new, but all with the same deadly result.

Pain. Injury. Death. That's all these mechanisms of war bring.

Around here, however, the people aren't likely to stand down without a fight. By the looks of things, many of the illegal vendors are packing, along with the various guards here to protect them and the market itself. Hidden inside stalls and behind heavy jackets, more weapons are swung to join the fight.

From inside the train, I spy many people firing back towards the far end of the old station, covering their retreats. Primarily, their weapons appear to be the older variety, their magazines stocked with only a certain capacity of bullets.

The enemy, meanwhile, will be carrying their pulse rifles and handguns, their energy clips and magazines capable of firing an almost continual barrage of red and blue rounds. In a battle of attrition, there's only one winner.

It only takes the Hawk a few seconds to quickly assess the surroundings. Walter stands to his side, holding a pulse gun of his own, looking out upon the carnage.

"Astor…we need to go!" he says to his guard, still peering out.

"Yes, sir. The north exit. Stay behind me. Both of you."

Following Astor out of the train, we immediately turn right, moving around the edge of the interior of the cavernous old station. I spare a glance behind, peering past tall pillars and the many stalls, and see the shape of the Con-Cops advancing, several dozen of them spreading in down the long tunnel I entered through.

But they're not alone. With them I spy others, the dark black-armoured figures of those I know to be Stalkers. They slash in, cutting a path into the hall at a devastating pace, quickly immobilising people as they attempt to flee or fight back.

Running onwards, we join a small group fleeing in the same direction. Panic spreads throughout the building, all available exits sought out by those with a more intimate knowledge of the area. Walter and Astor are clearly two such men, their place among the Nameless making this area of the city familiar to them.

Flashing his eyes backwards occasionally, and with his pulse rifle perpetually primed, Astor continues to drive us further towards the rear, Walter ushering me along and sticking close by. Soon enough, we're heading through a series of rooms and into another long passageway, retreating from the fighting through a network that to any other person might seem like a maze.

Pressing on, we reach a door and pass through onto the street, reaching the open air once more. I search left and right down the dimly lit alley, and see a few more shadows rushing away in either direction.

Customers escaping back to the safety of their other quarters. Merchants slipping away down streets they know well. Other Disposables, caught amid the fighting, trying to seek refuge as they sink deeper into the darkness of these forgotten streets.

Or at least that's what I thought. These streets

clearly aren't forgotten by the people here. By the Disposables who call them home. By the Nameless who use them to sneak around in the shadows. Even by the Con-Cops and the forces of Inner Haven, waging their unseen battle down here, behind the curtain and concealed from the general population.

Amid the fleeing shadows, however, others come seeking us out. As we move left, reaching a slightly wider street littered with derelict old buildings and rusty, antique cars, we catch sight of a fresh platoon of Con-Cops covering the rear of the station.

We switch direction, Astor's keen gaze helping us pace through the darkness at speed, our footfall slapping the concrete streets and creating a map of our presence that specialised Enhanced could follow. I've heard that *Bats*, with their supernatural sense of hearing, are quite capable of using nothing but their ears to determine the location of a single person across several city blocks, even if they're hidden out of sight.

All they need in a single footstep, and they can zero in on their quarry. And right now, all three of us are being extremely noisy as we run...

And that's to say nothing of *Sniffers*, our colloquial name for the Enhanced with an extraordinary sense of smell. The same sort of principle applies with them. Once they catch a scent, it can be pretty tricky evading them, particularly when they work in league with other Enhanced.

I can only imagine what a Stalker made from all those types of Enhanced would be like. Dashers and

Hawks and Sniffers and Bats. Maybe even throw in a bit of Brute blood for good measure.

Truly, they'd be unstoppable…

Still, there's nothing we can do but run, just like the many hundreds across the district. With so many sights and smells and sounds assaulting the senses of the Stalkers, we might just be able to sneak away unnoticed.

Or not.

As we come around a corner, I have no time to react as a flashing figure flows in from down the street, a blur of black as the man looms in front of me. Then another, storming in, weapon primed and ready to strike.

I stumble back, and notice Walter doing the same. Only Astor, with his keen eyes, is able to see them coming, lifting his weapon to send rounds of pulsing energy right at them.

But it's no good. They're too close, and too quick.

They dodge his blasts, swinging immobilisers from their belts as they come. With a couple of thrusts, Astor's body gets zapped. I sit helpless on the ground as sizzling darts of blue lightning appear to spread around his body, his limbs growing stiff and straight and his entire frame immobile.

Then, as he falls to the ground, eyes still narrow and searching, but body unable to move, the two Stalkers turn on Walter and me. For the first time, I get a good look at one of these hybrid hunters, their eyes dim behind their black helmets, their bodies wreathed in sleek black armour.

Both step forward, one towards me, the other towards Walter, brandishing their menacing rods as blue lightning dances around their ends. Neither of us are able to do anything, caught up by this sudden and devastating attack on the market, sweeping in and scooping up those who linger in the shadows of the city.

I wonder how many have been caught, or even killed. And for those who are merely snared in the net, who will be executed, and who will be sent for reconditioning?

I can think of few worse fates than being taken in and turned into a Con-Cop, or another servile slave of the state. If they find out I'm actually a hybrid, I'll no doubt be executed.

Personally, I'd prefer that than the alternative.

Caught at their feet with nowhere to go, I can do nothing but shut my eyes and wait to be zapped. I've heard being stung by an immobiliser is a horrible experience. Not painful, just horrifying.

With one tap, every muscle fibre on your body is turned rigid, every part of you locked in place in whatever position you happen to be adopting. But you don't lose consciousness. You merely have to endure your temporary paralysis, not knowing how long it will last, carted off like a living statue with your future presided over by those with no sense of compassion or empathy for your plight.

As the Stalker comes at me, I instinctively shut my

eyes, despite knowing that doing so will lock me into the darkness as well. But I'm unable to stop myself, ducking my head, closing up my body into a contorted, protective position that will no doubt be incredibly uncomfortable when fastened in place.

Eyes closed tight, I await the terrible zap, my heart rate flaring to unprecedented levels.

Nothing happens.

Are they toying with me? Will they spare me the torture of being immobilised?

A rush of air, flowing past my cheek, presents an answer. I can hear Walter exclaiming loudly to my side, and creak open my eyes to see that a third figure has appeared before us.

The flow of air signalled his introduction. He moves like a whirlwind, his body a blur as he tangles with the two Stalkers. I can barely make out what's happening before, suddenly, he stops and grows visible in front of my eyes.

And as he stands ahead of me with his back turned, the two Stalkers become visible too, collapsing into mounds of black armour on the concrete floor at his feet, knocked out cold.

The figure turns and reaches down to me, and I see the keen hazel eyes of Zander staring into mine.

"Hi there, Brie," he says casually.

"Zander…" I whisper. "How…how did you find me?!"

"Instinct," he says quickly, pulling me up to my

feet. "We'd better get you out of here. You too, Walter," he adds, turning to the chemist, who creakily stands from the dirt.

As he does so, Zander moves over and kneels down beside Astor. He conducts a quick check as Walter says: "He got zapped," as if that needed explaining.

I watch the proceedings, still feeling in a slight state of shock, my breathing hard and pulse soaring and body trembling in a way it's never done so before. I feel as if I might just pass out as I watch Zander pull out a little device from his belt and set one end to Astor's neck.

Shaped like a wide pen, Zander presses a button on the other end, and a little shock appears to pulse through Astor's body. The reaction is immediate, just as quick as that of the immobiliser. This particular device appears to offer an antidote, his limbs relaxing and eyes blinking and body coming back to life.

A *remobiliser...*

With a groan, he sits back up as Zander stands and moves back to me.

"Did they see you," he asks me, eyes fierce and probing.

"What do you mean..."

"Your face? Did they see your face? Did they recognise you?"

"I...I don't know."

Truly, I hadn't thought about it. In the heat of the moment, I wasn't exactly caring if they'd recognised me from the ceremony. But, now that I think about it, it could be important. Very important.

If they did, then I have no chance of going back to the academy. If they know who I am, and who I was with, then tonight has turned me into an outlaw.

A rebel.

A Nameless.

The reaction on my face makes my concerns clear to Zander.

"OK," he says, rounding on the two downed Stalkers. "It's not a problem. I can fix it."

"Fix it?" I ask. "You mean...kill them?"

"That's the *easiest* option," he says. "I'd shield your eyes, Brie…"

I shake my head.

"I've seen people die," I say defiantly. "I'm not afraid."

"Suit yourself," he says, withdrawing his own pulsar gun from a sheath on his belt.

He aims the weapon right at the heads of the two Stalkers, firing two blue shots of energy, one after another in quick succession. There's something methodical about his actions, the systematic murder of two men having no impact on him at all.

He turns back to me as I watch the blue haze fade around the freshly cut holes in their heads.

"Now what the hell are you doing here, Brie?! I told you to stay safe back at the academy!"

"I came looking for you. I *need* to know more, Zander! I need to know everything!"

His eyes soften a little, and a smile arches gently across his lips.

"And you will," he says. "But not here. We need to get off the streets. It's not safe around these parts, and you can be sure that two dead Stalkers will cause a fuss."

"Then where?" I ask.

His eyes sweep to the north, right towards the boundary of the city and the outside world beyond. And a single word issues from his mouth.

"Home," he says.

CHAPTER TWENTY FIVE

We venture further north, the fighting behind us growing distant to our ears. Around us, the streets grow darker than ever, a dead space with no functioning streetlights, no advertising boards.

Here, only the natural light of the moon and stars, or the occasional fire flickering down an alley, give shape to the buildings. A derelict portion of an otherwise flourishing city, left to rot by those in power.

Running alongside Zander, it becomes evident that his position among the Nameless has been fully confirmed, and Mrs Carmichael's concerns assuaged. He gets caught up with what happened from Walter and Astor, who tell him the attack was sudden and unexpected.

"They're growing more bold, more aggressive," says Walter. "It's escalation after the hijacking at the ceremony…"

"Someone must have talked, or been followed," says Astor. He glances at me, and I feel compelled to defend myself.

"I wasn't followed! And I certainly didn't talk!" I say.

Astor appears a little doubtful.

"You can trust her," says Zander authoritatively. "She's got more to lose by coming here than anyone."

We stop down a deserted street, and gather into a four. Zander pulls out a pair of goggles from his jacket and steps towards me.

"Put these on, Brie," he says.

I take them and place them over my face. Immediately, my vision is completely blocked, the world turning black.

"What's this about?" I ask. "I thought you said you trusted me!"

"It's not about trust," says Zander. "We can't have any outsiders knowing of our secret passages, not this far north."

"But I won't tell anyone!" I counter.

"I know you won't," he says, laying a hand on my shoulder. "But our enemy have powerful means of extracting information. It's best if, for now at least, you remain in the dark."

In the dark. Literally...

I choose not to argue, despite wanting to tear the goggles from my eyes as I'm led further on. In truth, all this has happened so fast I'm finding it impossible to keep up.

Perhaps Mrs Carmichael was right. Perhaps I should have just forgotten about all of this, gotten on with my simple life. Right now, I'm being led

284

towards something I don't properly understand, something I feel I have no control over at all.

And it's that total loss of control that I don't much like.

Now walking blind, I feel my other senses beginning to grow more attuned as we go. The sounds of our footsteps become more pronounced. The smell of the overgrown, rotting streets fills my nose, the changing of the air noticeable as we move through a secret door and enter into a passage.

Staying by my side, Zander guides me on, talking me through it when any obstacles come my way. Despite my quickly improving senses, my bearings are swiftly lost as we wind to the left and right, moving downwards towards the *underlands* of the city, the old tunnels and passages that were once part of the thriving metropolis that existed here.

Soon, my senses give shape to wider caverns as our footsteps echo louder, and the air seems to grow less dense, spreading out over a wide space. Other scents waft up my nose too, those of people and their odours. And the quiet sounds of talking filter into my ears, growing louder the further we progress.

"What is this place?" I ask as I gingerly make my way through the caverns and caves.

"Refuge," answers Zander.

"For who? The Nameless?"

"Anyone under the thumb of the Court. We give shelter to all those who'd see a terrible fate under their doctrine. Hybrids who'd be executed. Enhanced who want to escape Inner Haven. Unenhanced who have committed minor offences and would otherwise be reconditioned. All are given sanctuary here."

Soon, we're stopping once more, and saying goodbye to Walter and Astor.

"Thank you again, Zander, for your help," says Walter. His voice turns to me. "And you, Brie...I hope you find what you're looking for down here." I feel his hand take a light grip of my upper arm, and his voice lowers as he leans in. "Welcome to the cause," he says. "I'm sure you'll fit in just fine."

With that, I hear two sets of feet shuffle away as he and Astor move off. Alone now with Zander, I ask if I can take the mask off.

"Not yet, I'm afraid. We still have a little way to go."

We press on, continuing along passages that feel more narrow than the others. Interconnecting passages, perhaps, that link the larger caverns where these people come to seek safety from the Con-Cops and Stalkers who prowl the streets above.

I find myself asking if what happened this evening was a regular occurrence around here.

"Unfortunately, yes, and it's been getting worse recently. Platoons of Con-Cops often come here to mop up some of the Disposables, take them away to their secret facilities for reconditioning."

"To be made into more Con-Cops?" I ask. "Are

they building an army or something?"

"We don't know for sure," answers Zander. "But it's been more regular, and it's forced us to act. This is just the beginning…"

We continue on, and my mind now begins to flood with more questions. Questions about the Nameless, about what they're looking to achieve. I think back to the ceremony, and try to think of the words the man used.

He'd said a reckoning was coming. He's said the Fanatics were not who we thought they were.

"Who are they," I find myself asking out loud, my thoughts becoming vocal.

"Who?" asks Zander.

"The Fanatics. Something doesn't add up…the explosion the other day at the warehouse. What's really happening, Zander?"

With his hand on my arm, he stops dead in the quiet passage. I feel the urge to remove my goggles, and so reach up to pull them up onto my forehead. He doesn't object as I do so, my eyes first spying his, typically intense, and then the long passage stretching both ways into the darkness.

"You have a keen mind, Brie," he says, raising a little smile. "And it's only going to get keener. Tell me, what do your instincts say?"

I think for a moment, looking into the depths of his irises as if mining for information. And then the thought comes to me.

"They're being supported by the Court," I say. "They're people they've reconditioned. They're slaves."

He nods slowly.

"Yes," he says. "The Fanatics aren't just normal Unenhanced. They're not just zealots and radicals who believe that emotion is evil. They're people who have been conditioned to think that way, to act under the orders of the Savants. Most likely, they're Disposables who have been taken to their facilities and then sent back out to perform these atrocities…"

"But why? I don't understand. What are they looking to achieve?"

"Fear," answers Zander immediately. "It's a tool of suppression, a tool of control. We believe that the Savants have it in mind to spread their therapies, limit our liberties even further. Their experiments with Con-Cops and the Fanatics and their other slaves have proven to them that they can take a firmer grip on us. In time, we believe that they will remove emotion completely, suck the life right out of Outer Haven, and all those Enhanced living in Inner Haven too."

"So they've been behind it all along…" I say, shaking my head. "I guess, in a way, I'm not surprised. I mean, seeing Inner Haven for what it was, seeing all these people live without colour and art and culture. I suppose it was only a matter of time before they spread that thinking to us."

"Exactly. They've been doing it for years, trying different things, moving the chess pieces into place one by one. In the end, they want the people to volunteer for this, to make them more compliant. But if they don't manage that…they'll just force it on the people anyway."

"And who's behind all of this?" I ask. "Why now?"

"The Consortium determines this policy, as you know. But it's only grown worse in recent years since they elected their new leader."

"Director Cromwell?"

He nods.

"Director Cromwell is as callous a Savant as you'll find. His mission is simple: create a society of sheep, rebuild this world under his watchful eye. In the end, only those with something to offer will remain, with all those considered useless phased out or reconditioned to perform the tasks he deems important. With him at the helm, the human side of the city will gradually be lost. In the end, an entirely new species will emerge…"

I can hear the rising passion in his voice, see it in his eyes. This is clearly a fight he's been waging for many years, ever since he was a boy.

But for me…for me it's all new. Despite my curiosities and doubts, I never considered that such a plot was being perpetrated from within. Living in my blissful ignorance, I've spent my entire life in Outer Haven, knowing nothing of the truth.

Until now.

And tentatively, my voice rises into the cold, dark

passage with another question. Yet another part of this puzzle that I need to solve.

"And...why am I here?" comes my whisper.

Zander spreads his eyes down the passage again, right towards the deep blackness. Then he reaches forwards once more, and pulls the goggles back over my eyes.

"You're here, Brie, because you have a part to play in this," he says. He takes my arm again, and continues to lead me on. "Now come...she's waiting for us."

CHAPTER TWENTY SIX

Our path continues for quite some time. My knowledge of this area is so lacking that I have no idea how far away the boundary of the city truly is. And hidden behind these goggles, my perception of distance is most certainly hampered.

Eventually, the air begins to grow less stale, and the earth appears to rise a little. I consider that we must be nearing the end of our path, rising back up to the city streets and a new secret hideout.

When Zander stops me and removes my goggles, my suspicions are confirmed.

"Are we here?" I ask.

He nods, placing the goggles in his jacket pocket and drawing out what appears to be two gas masks. I frown as he passes me one, before drawing his own over his face. It's small and practical, covering only his nose and mouth and, presumably, allowing him to breathe in toxic environments.

"What's this for?" I ask.

His eyes dart towards a ladder next to us, leading up towards a little trap door.

"You'll see," he tells me. "Now put it on. It's more precautionary than anything."

I do as I'm told, hooking the mask to my nose and mouth and taking a breath. Then he moves straight for the ladder and climbs to the summit, disappearing through the trapdoor as I follow.

Emerging from the top, I look to see that I'm in what seems to be an old, wooden barn of some kind. The walls are broken down and cracked, the air carrying a light tinge of green to suggest its toxicity.

We move towards the barn door, and Zander pushes it open. As I follow him out my heart almost bursts from my chest, my eyes popping wide and stinging a little from the air. I tighten them up, but still look upon my surroundings with a gormless, slack jawed gape.

I'm outside the city.

In the distance, I can see it, shining like a beacon, the High Tower visible above it all and stretching skyward to the heavens. Around me are old derelict buildings, simple structures: little houses and barns and, ahead, an old church that looks to be more sturdily constructed.

It's towards the church that Zander leads me, my eyes now narrow to prevent the air from stinging too much. I suppose it can't be too damaging, otherwise we'd be wearing goggles. More dangerous to our respiratory systems, I guess, than anything else.

I continue to stare in all manner of directions as we press on, the moonlight casting down its glow upon this strange, ancient world. A village where people once lived, so long ago, before the world crumbled into the ash. Before vast swathes of it became uninhabitable.

Here, people must have lived simple lives, the world open for exploration, for travel. I often think of such times with no small amount of envy, when people could visit far flung lands and explore wild, untamed environments.

No longer.

Now, the only people who move beyond the boundaries of the city are those tasked with clearing the air of its toxicity, of making other lands safe for habitation.

I've heard many stories of workers dying from the toxic fog. Even their protective suits can fail to offer full protection from the mist.

Naturally, the concern boils up in me as we approach the church.

"Are we safe here?" I ask. "In this toxic air?"

"Perfectly," replies Zander casually. "This particular area is largely cleared."

His confidence settles my concerns as we reach the church door. He knocks loudly and with a distinctive pattern, the banging sound echoing out into the misty night. Then, moments later, the door creaks open and a man appears, dressed in lightweight armour and carrying a pulse rifle.

Stepping back, he opens the door wider, revealing the reinforced interior of the church, its windows barred and any old cracks and fissures in its façade sealed. Inside, various other guards sit or stand around, a force of hybrids most likely with all manner of special gifts. None wear gas masks, suggesting the church itself is fully sealed from outside.

As we enter, Zander pulls away his own mask, and I do the same, noting the many eyes watching me curiously as I advance.

"We heard the market was attacked," says the guard who gave us entry. "Did we lose many?"

"I don't know," answers Zander. "But it seemed to be worse than more recent attacks. I need to see *her* immediately."

The guard nods and continues to guide us towards the rear, where a second guarded door awaits. We're given passage inside, and enter into a short corridor with a third door at the end. As the door behind is shut off, leaving Zander and me momentarily alone, I feel a keen sense of nerves brewing.

"Who is this woman?" I ask. "And why was everyone staring at me?"

"They're just on high alert, think nothing of it. And this woman is one of the leaders of our cause."

"Leaders?! And why am *I* meeting *her*?!"

"Because she requested it," comes his swift response. "Don't look so nervous. If you can handle standing up in front of all of Inner Haven, you can handle this…"

He presses on and knocks on the door ahead. I wait, trying to control my breathing, but thinking myself completely unprepared for this and completely out of my depth.

So, sure, maybe I am a hybrid, and maybe a few abilities will manifest in me, but there appears to be dozens of hybrids around here. Maybe more. Hundreds, I don't know.

Why am I so special?

As my mind whirls, the door opens, and a warmth spreads from inside. I see a crackling fire giving off a comforting orange glow, the room carpeted in a warm maroon and far more inviting than the main part of the church behind us.

Zander steps in first, and I follow right behind, searching for this woman we're here to see. I turn to the window, and see a shadow looming, staring out over the cityscape beyond, at the High Tower soaring high and illuminated with a pale glow.

We stop before her, and a cool voice drifts towards us, calm and measured, her words deliberate.

"This must be the girl you've been telling me about, Zander."

"Yes, Lady Orlando. This is Brie Melrose."

The shadow turns, the light of the fire revealing her features. Dark eyes look upon me, searching and yet distant. Her face is pale and narrow, cheeks hollowed out and gaunt. There's a frailty to her frame, and yet a conviction in her face. I can't tell if she's welcoming or not, a smile rising on her face that leaves me confused.

"It's a pleasure to meet you, Brie," she says, stepping away from the window towards me. "Your performance at the ceremony was rather good, I thought."

"Um…thank you," I say, as she extends a bony hand.

I grip it and after a formulaic double shake, she slips her fingers from mine.

"I do apologise for interrupting your segment up there," she continues. "However, it was quite fortunate that you happened to appear before us all like that."

My confusion remains absolute. Now's the time for answers.

"Was it you?" I ask. "On the screen?"

"Oh…good God no, child. That was one of our many faithful warriors. The message, however, was something we all believe in."

"That the Fanatics are actually under the control of the Savants," I say.

"I see Zander's been informing you of things already."

"Well, actually Lady Orlando, she largely drew the conclusion for herself."

"I see. It's clear, however, that you remain in the dark about a great many things, Brie. I can see that your main question is simply…why are you here?"

I nod, and watch the smile continue to settle on her face, unmoving.

"Well, you, dear girl, are in a quite unique position

among our ranks."

Our ranks? It's as if she's already assimilated me right in...

"How so?" I ask.

"You are a unique mix, and potentially a special talent," she answers. "You have a power inside you that few have, as well as a position among the Unenhanced that presents a unique opportunity..."

"I...don't understand? What do you want me to do?"

She hovers over to a little side table by the fire, and pours herself a glass of whiskey. Clearly a favourite drink amongst the old ladies of this city.

In fact, the manner in which she's delaying reminds me a little of Mrs Carmichael. It's obvious that what they want from me isn't going to be easy.

Sipping her whiskey, she directs a question at Zander.

"Are you absolutely sure it's her?" she asks.

He looks at me, his endless gaze working its way right through me.

"I'm sure, Lady Orlando," he says.

She pours another two glasses of whiskey, and hands one to Zander, and then one to me.

"Take a sip, it'll calm you," she says. "I can see the concern in your eyes, Brie. But know this...you're not going to be forced to do anything you don't want to do. If you so wish, you can return to your academy and continue as you have been. If you choose to join us, however, you will need to know what you're getting yourself into."

Her words, and the sip of whiskey, do their job. I feel my body settling, my nerves being doused, the fire of fear and worry inside me slowly quenched.

These people killed my parents. I have no choice. I can't turn back.

I won't turn back.

My silence and the sudden calm in my demeanour draw a fresh smile onto Lady Orlando's face.

"Good," she says. "Now, I'm sure by now that Zander has informed you that the world you live in isn't quite what it seems. The Court have been working towards suppressing the liberties of the Unenhanced for many years. Truly, your visit to Inner Haven will have opened your eyes to the world they have created for themselves, and the Enhanced. It is their aim to make all lands under their rule as such…"

"Zander told me," I say, nodding. "I never knew it was so bad."

"Well, it is. However, we have no true idea of what their full intentions are. There are things that go on in the High Tower that none of us are privy to, and we've been looking for someone who can go to Inner Haven as a spy…"

As she speaks, my eyebrows descend lower and lower, and my features curl up with utter confusion.

"A spy," I find myself cutting in. I can't help it,

despite who I'm talking to. "You want me to be a *spy*! How can *I* do that?!"

"I understand your doubts, Brie. So let me explain. We have a man on the inside, a man who is currently unattached. He is due to attend a bachelor ball in the coming days, and with the impact you made during the ceremony, I'm sure we'll be able to get you to attend as well. As far as they know it, you're just an exceptional Unenhanced. It's the perfect cover."

"But…attend a bachelor ball…for the Enhanced? You have to be kidding me! So you want me to have a relationship with this man?"

"It will be nothing but a sham," comes Zander's voice. I find my eyes narrowing as I look at him. *This* is why he brought me here. "You'll be able to operate undercover in Inner Haven, and can help us from the inside. You'd be doing a world of good, Brie…"

"But why me?! I mean, what can I offer? How could I possibly get into the High Tower?!"

A million other queries and concerns materialise in my head as Zander and Lady Orlando share a look.

"Settle yourself, Brie," says Lady Orlando. "Take another sip of whiskey. It helps, it really does."

I do as ordered, taking a moment to compose myself.

"Now, we understand this is all a bit of a shock," she continues. "That is only natural. However, as you well know, it is common for Unenhanced to marry into the ranks of the Enhanced, and live in Inner Haven. With your profile as it is, and the hidden abilities inside you, we consider you a prime candidate to take on this mission…"

"But I'm no spy, and I don't even know what abilities I'll have, if any! And, what if they find me? What if they discover that I'm a hybrid? I'll be killed…"

Once more, my voice quickens, forcing Zander to slide in beside me and offer me a comforting arm. As he does so, I hear Lady Orlando whispering quietly to him.

"Tell her, Zander. She needs to know. I'll give you some space."

I raise my eyes again to see the old lady shift towards the door. Before she leaves, she offers a final few words to me.

"You are compelled to do nothing, Brie. Remember that. You can forget all of this, if you want, and return to your world. The choice, really, is yours."

With that, she opens the door and slips out of the room, leaving Zander and me alone once again. I find the whiskey glass back at my lips, my desire for a refill quickly growing stronger.

Zander seems to sense such a thing. The bottle is sought and a fresh supply emptied into my glass. After returning the bottle to the table, he wanders slowly over towards the window, his eyes set on the distant shape of the High Tower, glowing in the darkness.

A short silence follows, before his voice registers in the room once more, softer this time, more calm.

"My mother once lived there," he says, gazing into the night.

The words take a moment to register.

"Your mother…was a Savant?" I ask, still standing by the fire.

I see his head nod, his body so still. I wonder how far his eyes can take his gaze, whether he can make out the details of the High Tower, see the shadows of shapes moving within.

"My mother had strange powers that she passed to me. I can see into people's minds, Brie, read and manipulate their thoughts. For a long time, I was like you, hidden in Outer Haven, my abilities suppressed. Then, my life changed one day, and I found myself on this path. It's one I've trodden since I was just a boy…"

I find myself moving towards him, drawn in as he speaks. There's a melancholy to his words, a suppressed sadness and simmering anger, locked down below the surface.

As I come, nearing his side, I whisper into the now quiet room: "You're a Mind-Manipulator?"

"I'm many things," he says. "Many things, like you…"

I reach him and turn my eyes to his, still fixed to

the distance and refusing to blink.

"But how do you know? How do you know what I am?" I ask, my voice little more than a murmur now.

His hand slips into his jacket. His fingers withdraw a piece of card, folded in two. Finally, he turns to me, opening the card up before his eyes.

"I know what you are, Brie…I know what you can do…because you can do what I can. We're one and the same. And when I saw you, on that big screen, I finally knew…I'd found you…"

His words come out slowly as he opens the card, twisting it around to show me the other side.

My breathing halts. My heart-rate suddenly grows stiff. My eyes lock to the picture, to the image of my parents, looking down at their child.

But not one child.

Two.

Then, slowly, my eyes lift again and meet with Zander's. Hazel, like mine, deep as an ocean. And a smile forms on his face.

"You and me…we're twins, Brie."

The Enhanced will continue in Book Two...

To hear about the author's latest discounts and
new releases, sign up to his newsletter at
www.tcedgebooks.com

49137725R00171

Made in the USA
San Bernardino, CA
14 May 2017